MIDNIGHT GODS

GREG F. GIFUNE

JOURNALSTONE
YOUR LINK TO ARTIST TALENT

JournalStone books may be ordered through booksellers or by contacting:

JournalStone

www.journalstone.com

The views expressed in this work are solely those of the authors and do not necessarily reflect the views of the publisher, and the publisher hereby disclaims any responsibility for them.

ISBN: 978-1-947654-30-3 (sc)
ISBN: 978-1-947654-31-0 (ebook)

JournalStone rev. date: May 4, 2018
1st Edition

Library of Congress Control Number: 2018940692

Printed in the United States of America

Cover Design: Augusto "Ace" Silva at BlesseD´Signs / 99designs
Interior Layout: Jess Landry

Proofread by Scarlett R. Algee
Edited by Vincenzo Bilof

ACKNOWLEDGMENTS

Thanks to my wife Carol, and to my family, friends, fans and readers all over the world for their continued support. And thanks to my brother-from-another-mother and colleague Dave Thomas, for taking the first look at this one, and providing me with invaluable feedback.

For Eric Shapiro, who once, as I lay dying and riddled with bullets on the causeway, in his wisdom, reminded me that *"Tattaglia's a pimp. He never could've outfought Santino."* This one's for you, brother.

MIDNIGHT GODS

"The enemy is fear. We think it is hate; but, it is fear."

—Gandhi

PART ONE

"A surprising number of human beings are without purpose, though it is probable that they are performing some function unknown to themselves."

—Cliff Green, *Picnic at Hanging Rock* (screenplay)
From the novel by Joan Lindsay

1

They should've never been in the car that night. The party was still going on, but they'd left abruptly, and earlier than expected. Full and unusually bright, the moon cast the darkness in a strange and otherworldly glow, and although it was nearly ten o'clock, a thin veil of fog blanketed the area, drifting ghostlike all around them. Had they not known better, they'd have thought it dusk. In fact, visibility was so high and the moon so bright, headlights barely seemed necessary.

Oliver offered to drive but Emily insisted on taking the wheel. Even after he voiced his concerns, suggesting that perhaps he was in better shape to drive since he'd only had a couple drinks to her three or four, and was also far less agitated, she maintained, in no uncertain terms, that she was more than capable of getting them home without incident. After all, it was less than five miles from Will and Nora's place to theirs, she reminded him, stopping outside their Impala to light a cigarette. Her anger was not in question at that point, Oliver just wasn't sure how much of it, if any, was directed at him. Emily rarely allowed herself fits of outright rage, but when she did, she unleashed it like a napalm strike.

Everything burned.

Oliver remembered looking at her over the roof of the car. Watching her, really, assessing her, he supposed, the night so quiet it made him suspicious. A slight breeze kicked up, as if from nowhere, out of place on such an otherwise still and chilly night. Emily's hair danced briefly as the breeze rushed past, and she stood there, taking deliberate and deep drags on her cigarette, one after the next in a manic fashion. Gazing off into the night like she'd noticed something he hadn't, she never looked his way. Oliver found that odd, since he was sure she knew he was staring at her.

"Do you want to talk about it?" he asked.

"Not particularly."

He dropped into the passenger seat without another word.

Emily remained outside the car until she'd finished her cigarette. Oliver wasn't sure exactly how long that took, but it seemed forever, like the world had paused, waiting for them to wander off into the tapestry of such a peculiar and mysterious night and all the secrets hidden within it.

When the door opened and she finally got in, settling behind the wheel before quickly checking the mirrors and turning the ignition, she appeared harried and not quite sure of herself as before.

"I'm happy to drive," Oliver said.

"I got it," she answered breathlessly, sweeping a wisp of auburn hair from her eyes. "Just wanted to clear my head, stop making a big deal about it. I really don't need you adding to my aggravation at this point, okay?"

"I didn't know Arthur was going to be there."

"Isn't he always? *God*, he's such an insufferable douche bag."

Oliver reached over and switched the radio off. Looking back now, he couldn't remember what was playing, but he didn't want her distracted. "Why Will and Nora insist on inviting him to these get-togethers is beyond me. I understand he and Will have been friends since high school, but—"

"From now on, if Arthur's there, we won't be."

"Yes," Oliver agreed. "He clearly delights in causing trouble and instigating arguments."

"Particularly with me, and I'm tired of it."

"Well, you set him straight."

"Ignorant windbag misogynist goon had it coming." She checked herself in the rearview quickly, as if more from habit than necessity. "I'll give Nora a call tomorrow and apologize for losing it like that in front of everyone and storming out, but enough is enough."

"The look on Arthur's face was priceless. He wasn't expecting you to go off on him like that. I'm sure he wanted an argument, it was fairly obvious that's what he'd come looking for. He's not exactly subtle, but you annihilated him. First time I've ever seen that loud-mouth speechless."

Emily finally looked at him, her big brown eyes feral and passionate in the dashboard glow. "I noticed you came right to my defense," she said.

"When have you ever needed defending?"

She seemed to think about that a moment. "It's not about need."

"You're right. I'm sorry. I guess I didn't want to escalate things."

"No, of course you didn't."

Since she was still looking at him, Oliver risked a slight smile. "You want I should go back in there and punch him in his big stupid face?"

Something shifted in her expression that let him know her anger was softening. "Did I make an ass of myself?"

"Not at all, sweetheart."

"Would you tell me if I had?"

"Not at all, sweetheart."

Emily laughed lightly then dropped the car into drive. "With all that's going on in the world these days, I've had all I can stand of fascist garbage."

"Arthur was out of line. He always is. You did the right thing."

Without answering she pulled away, and they headed down the street to the avenue at the head of the block. Oliver sat back and tried to relax, watching the night and fog move past them, headlights cutting the limited darkness ahead.

Deserted, the main street in town, such as it was, looked unusually eerie. Everything had closed at least an hour before, and the area was desolate and quiet, a ghost town on a cold and bright winter night. Filthy ice and snow packed along the gutters, remnants of a storm a week earlier, drew Oliver's attention. It was always the last to go, this once pristine and glistening snow, dirty, dying and pushed aside until it mutated into something other than originally intended. There was something familiar to him about these narrow swaths of crystalline ice, black as soot and lining the curbs by design, though not in a typical sense.

It's us, he thought. *Sooner or later, it's all of us.*

Oliver was still contemplating that when he first saw the man.

Up ahead, a lone figure stood at the edge of the sidewalk to his right, facing the street. Definitely male, tall and thin and clad in a long coat to his ankles; a black fedora atop his head, the man stood in profile, wrapped in fog. His silhouette was striking and unnaturally still, like something manufactured, a black cutout of a person positioned and left there for some unknown reason rather than a flesh-and-blood being. The man never looked their way, so Oliver assumed he had no plans to cross the street, and even if he had, surely it would be once they'd passed by.

Emily must have assumed the same, as she initially slowed the car upon seeing him, and then continued on when he neither gave a look in their direction nor made any move whatsoever.

Oliver felt he should say something, though the words, if he ever truly possessed them, refused to come. This strange and urgent need to voice something—anything—in that moment, struck him as more instinctual than logical in nature, so rather than dismiss it, he let his mouth drop open, hopeful something of value might emerge.

"*Emily*," he heard himself say.

It was then the silhouette stepped from the curb, directly into their path.

"Jesus!" Emily gasped.

The car swerved violently, and Oliver was thrown against the door, his head striking the window with enough force to cause an explosion of white then blue light. Like the flash of a camera, it expanded as a flower might when blooming rapidly, filling his entire field of vision and concealing what he thought for a brief second was the blurred face of the man on the other side of his window.

Void of features, it was a face of shadows, a face not quite... finished.

Not quite human.

And then there came the unnatural sound of the car coming into contact with something that should not have been there. A dull thud followed by a vague scraping sound, the screech of tires and finally...silence.

"My God," Oliver said, straightening up and pawing at his eyes. "What—"

"He stepped right in front of us!" Emily looked in the rearview, her face a mask of shock and disbelief. "I—by the time I realized what he'd done it was too late!"

Oliver realized they were still moving. Albeit slowly, just a creep really, but Emily had not come to a complete stop. "Did you hit him?" he asked, even though he knew the answer. "Is he all right, is—"

"I just clipped him, I—I barely touched him, I swerved at the last moment and missed him, I—I think I mostly missed him!"

Mostly missed him, he thought, *what an absurd thing to say.*

Oliver turned and looked back over the seat through the rear window.

The man was on the ground.

"Pull over," he said dully.

She didn't.

"For Christ's sake, Emily, pull over, we have to—"

"I think he's all right, I—"

"Pull over! You have to pull over!"

"Look!"

The man slowly regained his feet, appeared to wipe himself off, then straightened his coat. After a second or two, he reached down and retrieved his fedora, which had been knocked off in the fall. Placing it carefully on his bald head, he adjusted it, pulling the brim down in front as he'd worn it previously.

And then, for the first time, he turned and looked right at them.

"He—He's fine," Emily said, "he's okay, look, he's—"

"Goddamn it, pull over!"

Emily kept driving, still moving at a snail's pace, but moving nonetheless, inching closer and closer to the turnoff that would take them back home and leave all this behind.

The man remained in the middle of the street, watching them, but Oliver still couldn't make out any features. He was shadows, nothing more.

"We're going home," Emily said, "he's all right."

Oliver reached out and gently touched her arm. Maybe she was in shock. Maybe they both were. "Sweetie, we just hit a man with the car, you—you need to stop, we need to make sure he's all right and—"

"What? Call the police?"

"I don't know, I—"

"We've both been drinking, Oliver."

"We have to stop."

"I just clipped him, it's not like I ran him down. He's fine."

"We don't know that, we have to—"

"We're getting out of here."

Oliver watched as the shadow in the middle of the street, still as a statue once again, receded into darkness and fog.

2

The house was dark. Oliver distinctly remembered leaving a light on over the sink in the kitchen when they'd left for the party, but the only bulb burning was one in an outside fixture mounted to the side of the front door.

Emily pulled into the driveway alongside their SUV and turned the car off. They sat there a while, listening to the night and the rapid, frenzied cadence of their breath. They both wanted to say things, needed to probably, but neither did.

Oliver noticed Emily's hands shaking as she tried to light another cigarette. After several failed attempts, he took the lighter from her hand and ignited it, holding the flame steady as she leaned in and got it going.

Emily's face, bathed in sinister flame, looked oddly demonic. As her eyes lifted to meet his, he extinguished the lighter. He didn't want to see her like that.

They left the car and walked the winding stone path to the front door, shuffling along mindlessly. Like zombies. Cigarette dangling from her lips, Emily stabbed a key in the lock as Oliver stepped deeper into the pool of light over the door, hopeful it would provide even minimal comfort from the fear and tension coursing through him.

Theirs was one of three houses on a small cul-de-sac that was set back from the main road and surrounded by forest. For the first time since they'd left Main Street, Oliver allowed himself to look back in the direction from which they'd come. He studied the end of their road for signs. Of what, exactly, he wasn't sure, though passing before his mind's eye he had visions of the man, having followed them, appearing in the darkness like a phantom, standing there and watching them, still and silent and frightening.

But there was nothing there, no one.

A soft crackling sound emanated from the woods behind them as something unseen scurried through the trees, and Oliver was gripped by the sudden sensation that something was lumbering through the forest, rushing up behind them, snapping branches as it went.

As Emily pushed open the door and slipped into the waiting kitchen, Oliver followed, closing the door behind them before locking it then checking the knob to make certain it wouldn't budge. He switched the outside light off then thought better of it and turned it back on.

What seemed to be an inordinate amount of mail was sprawled across the kitchen table. Magazines, bills, small unopened packages and junk strewn in great piles covered the entire surface. A few pieces had fallen to the floor as well. Oliver stared at the mess a moment, considered going through it then decided against it. Instead, he pulled off his jacket, hung it on a hook on the wall then watched as Emily made her way to the sink. She ran the water and leaned forward, her back to him, head hanging and forearms resting on the counter.

Oliver crossed the room, turned the light on over the sink he swore he'd left on when they left, then noticed the clock on the stove to his right.

10:45.

Distracted by a soft noise escaping his wife, something between a sigh and a whimper, he put his hand on the small of her back and rubbed gently.

"Do you think we'll have any trouble?" Emily asked without looking at him.

"I don't know. Probably not, I—I don't think so, no."

"You were right. I should've stopped."

Oliver collected two glasses and a bottle of bourbon from a nearby cupboard. "It's over now," he said.

Emily straightened up and turned her back to the sink, hands on either side of her bracing the counter as if fearful she might slide to the floor otherwise. She looked devastated, like she'd sustained a horrible beating and had just then groggily awakened from it. "Is it?"

"Yes." Oliver poured her a drink, then one for himself.

"What if he followed us?"

"Followed us?"

"Yes, what if he followed us here?"

"He was on foot, Emily."

"What if he got our license plate?"

"By the time he got up we were quite a distance away," he reminded her. "I doubt seriously he could've seen our plate by then."

"He knows the make, model and color of our car."

"It's just as likely he only knows it was a silver car. There are a lot of silver cars in town, and besides, even if he recognized the make, we're not the only ones around here who own a silver Impala."

"But what if—"

"Here," Oliver said, offering her the drink. "It'll make you feel better."

"What if this isn't over?" she asked, her bottom lip trembling. "What if—"

"Take it," he said, pressing the glass into her hand. The same thoughts had been firing through his head on an endless loop since the incident took place, but he didn't want her to know that, so Oliver did his best to appear calm.

Emily took several hard drags on her cigarette, staring down into the amber liquid as if it held answers, perhaps salvation. "I should've stopped. Why didn't I stop? I—I was so scared, it—I panicked and I wasn't thinking straight, I—I should've stopped."

"But we didn't," Oliver said, making sure he emphasized *we*. "He was all right. Probably shaken up, likely has bumps and bruises, but he was all right."

Emily brought the glass to her lips and slid the liquor down her throat in a single gulp. She held her eyes closed a moment then said, "You really think so?"

"Yes, I do. He was back on his feet and standing just fine on his own power. If he'd been hurt he would've stayed down." Oliver sipped his drink, drifted over toward the den, switched on another light.

"Turn that off!"

"Why?"

"If he's out there he can see in if the lights are on!"

"Emily, he's not out there. Main Street's more than three miles from here. Even if he knew exactly where we live—and he doesn't—he'd still be walking and more than a couple miles away."

She stared at him, eyes drained of everything but fear.

Oliver switched off the light.

"What a nightmare," she said quietly. "What an awful, awful nightmare."

"Why don't you go lay down for a while?"

Emily put her glass in the sink, pulled her coat off and threw it over the back of a kitchen chair. "Yes, I think I will. Maybe I'll take a bath."

Oliver plucked what remained of the cigarette from her lips and tossed it into the sink. It died with a hiss as it hit a small puddle near the drain. "Go relax," he said, kissing her on the lips then forehead. As their eyes met, he was certain hers was the saddest expression he'd ever seen. He wondered if she saw the same in him. He summoned the best smile he could. "I'm going to stay up a bit."

Once she'd reached the doorway to the hallway that would lead her to the staircase, Emily hesitated. "I didn't mean to hurt him. I never saw him."

"I know, sweetheart."

"I did my best to avoid him."

"Emily, I know."

"I panicked, I—"

"We both did. Look, I feel terrible about this too, but it was an accident."

"You weren't driving."

He wasn't sure how to answer that, so he didn't.

"Maybe we should go back," she said.

"I don't think that's a good idea."

"Why?"

"Because I'm sure he's gone by now."

"You can't know that."

"Besides, we..."

She knew what he was going to say because she was thinking the same thing. They'd left the scene of a crime. A hit and run, that's what it was, and whether the man was injured or not, they'd broken the law. For God's sake, they'd struck a human being with their car and left the scene without stopping.

Just the same, Oliver knew his wife. He knew himself. They would've stopped had it been an animal. So why had they kept going? Why had Emily instinctually fled the scene when doing the exact opposite was clearly more in line with who she really was?

"What was he doing out there in the first place?" she asked suddenly. "I never got a close look at him, but the way he was dressed makes me think he was an older man."

"Yes," Oliver said, "I think so too."

"What was an old man doing out in the dark and fog at this hour?"

"Going for a walk, maybe? I don't know."

Even in the limited light, Oliver could see her eyes were moist, and her eyeliner had begun to run in skinny lines across her cheeks. "Christ," she said, wiping smudges from her face with the back of her hand. "What have I done?"

"Nothing, it was an accident followed by some innocent poor judgment on both our parts. That's all."

"I might've killed him."

"But you didn't. I'm telling you, he's fine."

"I feel so *tired*, I...."

"Adrenaline dump," Oliver said. "It's to be expected after all this."

"It's something more. Something's *wrong*."

"Everything's all right," he assured her.

"No," she said, disappearing into the darkness of the hallway. "It's not."

3

Somewhere far off, a siren wailed then gradually faded.

The quiet returned, but Oliver's nerves still hadn't yet settled.

Collapsed in a chair in the den, he sat sipping his drink in the dark. He didn't know why he hadn't turned on any lights; it just felt right, as if he needed to hide in the safety the darkness provided, prey huddled in the shadows, away from the light and reach of the predatory eyes hunting him. Normally he'd have dismissed such odd thoughts as melodramatic nonsense born of an overactive imagination. But this night was different. On this night, it seemed to Oliver, virtually anything was possible. He couldn't turn the television or radio on without seeing violence and anger tearing the globe apart, people across the country full of hate for one another. Rage, such unbridled *rage*, and all of it infecting the world like the disease it was, pulling everyone down into the gutter with the filth, where dead things collected and rotted, and those creatures that fed upon mankind huddled like the gleeful conspirators they were, hoarding their useless trophies of hopelessness and decay, false righteousness and perceived victory, muttering lies and gazing out across a manufactured reality with eyes long blind.

The world had gone mad long ago, of course, but Oliver had mistakenly thought them immune somehow. He believed he and Emily could weather these terrible storms of politics and war, hatred and division, intolerance and cruelty, this constant struggle between those trying desperately to cling to things no one else wanted, and those arrogantly rushing toward a future they were so certain could be nothing but superior, if only the rest of the world saw things exactly as they did.

He remembered Arthur and Emily at the party earlier, going at it from different ends of the political spectrum, and while Oliver believed his wife was right, at least to the logical extent that he agreed with her, the level of anger both she and Arthur had shown each other was astonishing. He didn't know much about Arthur, other than he was an old friend of Will's. He'd worked with Will for years, and he seemed to have virtually nothing in common with Arthur. On more than one occasion, Nora had mentioned she couldn't stand him. Yet he was always around, and while frankly Oliver didn't care a great deal about him, he did care about Emily. He cared about…

The Emily you care about would stop if she hit a pedestrian with her car.

His mind replayed the incident, but there were already pieces missing. *Had* they stopped? At one point, had the car stopped rolling, creeping and slinking away from the scene like the guilty thing it was?

He couldn't remember, but it was possible. Wasn't it? Could Emily be right? *Was* there something more to this, a piece of this nightmare that was continuing to elude them, existing in the periphery, just beyond their memory?

Here it was after eleven, and he remembered that the clock read 10:45 when they'd arrived home. Yet they'd left the party just before 10:00. Hadn't they? If so, that meant it took them an hour to get home. That couldn't be right, wasn't possible. He must have been mistaken about the time they'd left Will and Nora's. He had to be. But sitting there, alone with his thoughts, it didn't feel that way. It didn't feel that way at all.

Pipes rattled overhead. Oliver looked up, as if expecting to see something more than ceiling and shadows. With a weary grunt, he rose from the chair, left his empty glass on the coffee table and crossed the den to the stairs. Evidently, Emily hadn't turned any lights on upstairs either, as the steps and landing above were cloaked in darkness.

With a quick look back over his shoulder, he glanced through the windows on the far wall at what he could see of the front yard. The front light, still on, only reached about a quarter of the yard beyond the walkway, but Oliver could see enough that he was satisfied no one was there.

Just as he was about to take the stairs, something stopped him.

Slowly, he looked back at the windows, and realized he'd begun to drift toward them.

Oliver froze, his eyes adjusting and shifting, alternating between his dark reflection in the glass and the night beyond. He watched his face looking back at him, gone then there again like a troubled ghost fading in and out of existence. Squinting, he focused on the darkness on the other side of the thin pane of glass, the only thing separating *in here* from *out there*.

Nothing but night...

And yet, he was gripped with the horrible, strangling feeling that someone was watching him. Someone not so very far away, but perhaps positioned on the other side of the driveway, standing in the darkness between the trees.

Can you feel me?

That terrible thudding sound echoed in his mind.

Can you feel me watching you?

A featureless face gliding past the car window flashed in his mind.

Can you feel me inside you?

Eyes clenched shut, Oliver waited until the visions and sensations retreated.

When he opened his eyes a moment later, slowly and partially, like a child peeking out over covers pulled up tight to his chin, he realized there was nothing there. No phantom, no old man in a fedora.

No, he thought, *of course not.*

Turning his back to the windows, he crossed to the stairs and climbed them, moving through the darkness and silence as if by rote.

After negotiating a short hallway, and ignoring the photographs in dusty frames decorating the walls on either side of him, Oliver slipped into their bedroom.

Moonlight through the windows illuminated enough for him to see the bed. It was unmade, the sheets and blankets all kicked into a tangle near the foot. It looked as if it hadn't been properly made or even straightened in days.

A vague flicker of light at the rear of the bedroom drew his eyes to the door to the master bathroom. It stood ajar.

Emily was likely still having her bath, and from what little he could make out through the cracked door, she'd lit candles and positioned them about the bathroom, as she often did when soaking in the tub.

"Sweetie?" he said, voice so soft he couldn't be sure he'd really spoken.

Just then he saw himself in the mirror over her bureau, a murky figure lurking near their bed, arms at his sides and shoulders slouched as if burdened with an immense weight. Straightening his posture, Oliver watched his reflection stand taller and move closer, his eyes black sockets on a pale canvas laced with shadow. He reached for the mirror, to be certain it truly *was* his reflection, and not some ghoul.

Their fingers touched, but he'd never felt more alone.

Something shifted, moved behind him, something that separated from the darkness and glided quickly from sight.

Turning, he looked behind him at the doorway, and inadvertently stepped into the beam of moonlight. His eyes followed it to the night from which it came. The full moon hung low in the sky, enormous and brilliant before him like an indifferent deity at the height of its power and majesty.

Mesmerized, Oliver stood motionless, unable to take his eyes from it.

A gentle splashing sound escaped from the partially open bathroom door. He heard it again, and then a third time, but it wasn't until the fourth or fifth occurrence that he finally looked in its direction.

Oliver took hold of the door and pushed it open.

Candles burned, their flames licking the walls and floor, flickering and casting the otherwise dark room in a fiery, spooky glow. Emily sat in the tub, knees pulled up against her chest, arms wrapped around her calves, her petite body nude and shivering, glistening with a slick sheen of peculiarly tinted water.

"Emily?" he said, not sounding quite so distant this time. "Are you okay?"

She turned her head, rested her cheek on top of her knees, and looked at him. Her eyes blinked. Slowly, the way a reptile's might.

But it was the water that bothered Oliver. There was something wrong with it…with the color…

Blood. There was blood in the water. Slinking along the surface and slick like oil, it spiraled deeper, burrowing beneath and soaking into her bare flesh.

"Emily?" he said again.

She rose to her feet and stepped from the tub, crimson trickling and snaking across her body in tiny rivulets. Draped in flickering candlelight, Emily closed the gap between them, padding silently across the tile floor.

Without taking her eyes from him, she slowly closed the door.

4

In the dream, he was a kid again, just nineteen and back in his freshman year of college. 1992. Twenty-five years ago now, and yet, even in dreams it seemed like another lifetime entirely, a separate place and time void of context, experienced by some alternate version of himself, or perhaps a cunning imposter living on borrowed time and stolen memories.

Boston. Boylston Street. Marty's, a small used record store in an attic space above a Chinese takeout, a little hole-in-the-wall few knew about where albums of every description were displayed in boxy bins and old milk crates along the floor, the walls covered in concert posters. CDs had become the rage, and records were already a thing of the past. While Oliver appreciated the clarity of the new format, he loved vinyl and still played records. Records seemed more human to him, flawed and deep and rich. They had soul. He still bought them whenever he could, and Marty's had become a favorite haunt of his, a place he could find older and used albums at low prices. Hardly anyone wanted them anymore, so for someone like Oliver, it was a goldmine.

His dreams took him there, back to the day he first saw Emily.

He was checking out a copy of Gary Wright's 1975 album *The Dream Weaver* when he first noticed her, a petite girl with big brown eyes and auburn hair flipping through the stacks a few rows away.

The James Taylor tune *Something in the Way She Moves* was playing from a pair of old speakers on the counter, and from that moment forward, Oliver would always think of her when he heard that song.

Except for the clerk behind the counter, a bored middle-aged guy reading a copy of *The Stranger* by Albert Camus, they were the only two in there, and while Oliver tried numerous times to catch her eye, she didn't seem to notice him at all.

Pretending to do so casually, Oliver drifted over to her row. It was *adult contemporary* stuff; Frank Sinatra, Judy Garland, Tony Bennett, Sammy Davis Jr., music his parents listened to. He'd known the moment he saw her there was something different about her, so it only stood to reason she'd be into music most kids their age paid little attention to. This quirk only made Oliver want to know her more, so he flipped through a few albums and acted as if he had an idea of what he was looking for.

"Who's your favorite?" she asked suddenly.

He pretended he'd just noticed her as well. "I'm sorry?"

"Singer, I mean." She motioned to the albums before them. "Who's your favorite?"

Oliver looked into those big beautiful eyes and fell right into them, melting away like some love-struck puppy. "I, ah...um..."

Falling...

Oliver.

First to light...

Oliver!

...and then to darkness...

Oliver, wake up!

He smiled at her, and she smiled back.

Her teeth were stained with blood.

Oliver!

So much blood...

Oliver, wake up!

The past crumbled away with the inelegance of toppled ruins, and Oliver found himself in their bedroom, stretched out on the edge of the bed. Apparently at some point he'd decided to lie down a moment and slipped off to sleep. As his eyes focused and deciphered the shadows and moonlight, he realized someone was there, next to the bed.

The man in the fedora stood over him, the brim pulled down

so Oliver couldn't make out his face. Wheezing and groaning like some impossibly old and diseased *thing*, his voice a deep gurgling sound, he mumbled what sounded like prayers or chants in a language Oliver didn't recognize.

His hands protruded from the cuffs of his long dark coat, pale and bony appendages; fingers unfurling to reveal thick, long, curved claw-like things that more closely resembled talons than fingernails.

The tips sparkled in the moonlight.

Like razors.

Clicking them together in what was a horrifying and merciless sound, he raised his arms from his sides and spread them wide, the coat pulling away to form what looked like two giant wings protruding from either side of his torso. A profane hybrid of man and bat, the man stood before him, arms fully extended and head bowed, but Oliver couldn't determine if this was the posture of a predator preparing to strike, or simply a maneuver to showcase his grandeur and power, a reminder that he could take him whenever he chose to do so, and there was nothing Oliver could do to stop him.

The street…the cold…the darkness in the alleys between buildings and along the tops of the trees…something moving up there, in the night sky…

Instinctually, Oliver reached out, as if to push him away, and tried to sit up, but he was frozen with fear. He struggled to scream for help, the words dying in his throat, little more than strangled, pathetic whimpers.

Something moving closer…walking as a man, but not a man…not a man at all…coming closer…

"Oliver!"

Go! Drive! Go! Don't stop! Don't—

Oliver blinked and the man was gone, folded back into the shadows he'd been born of. The horrible sounds and visions faded as well, and instead it was Emily hovering over the bed in her bathrobe, her face twisted into a grimace of terror.

Shaking him by the shoulders, she frantically said Oliver's name again and again in a loud whisper. "Oliver! Oliver, wake up!"

"Dreaming," he said, his voice slurred. "I think…I think I was… *dreaming*."

"Wake up!" Emily hissed, shaking him again, harder this time.

Oliver stared into her terrified eyes until he was certain it was really her. Forcing himself into a sitting position, he scanned the room, but still wasn't sure he was fully awake. "What is it?" he asked. "What's wrong?"

"There's someone downstairs," Emily whispered, her grip on his shoulders tightening. "There's someone in the house!"

Her words registered and he was awake and on his feet instantly, trying to get his bearings and staggering about like a fool. "Are you sure?"

"I heard someone moving around downstairs," she insisted.

"You didn't dream it?"

"I wasn't asleep. You were."

Oliver listened a moment. The house was dead silent.

"Stay here," he told her, crouching and grabbing the baseball bat he kept under the bed. He noticed her phone on the nightstand. "If you hear things escalate, call 911."

Emily nodded rapidly and snatched up her phone.

He crept into the hallway, moved though the darkness to the top of the stairs. Hesitating, he listened again but heard nothing. He flipped the switch on the wall.

Light flooded the staircase and landing below.

There was no one there, and despite the sudden intrusion of light, Oliver heard no sudden noises or reactionary sounds of movement. He thought about maybe calling out then decided against it. Part of him wanted to go back into the bedroom, lock the door, call the police and let them handle this, but like so much else to do with this strange night, he wasn't sure if he had complete control over any of it.

Oliver looked back over his shoulder.

Emily stood in the bedroom doorway, watching him, phone in hand. In the dark, she looked pale and terrified. He remembered the bloody bathwater and her sullen expression as she closed the door.

Heart jackhammering his chest, Oliver tightened his grip on the bat, and slowly descended the stairs.

5

Oliver held his position at the foot of the stairs and tried to see as far as the light allowed. Emily had never been prone to flights of fantasy, so he tried to prepare himself for the very real possibility that someone had broken into their home and was lurking in the shadows, perhaps even watching him at that very moment. He listened, taking shallow breaths through his mouth so as to make as little noise as possible.

The house was quiet.

Creeping, Oliver crossed the den, turning on lights as he went.

When he'd reached the kitchen he could hear the steady hum of the refrigerator, nothing more. Reaching around the doorframe to the switch, he turned on an overhead fixture and the kitchen appeared before him as if by magic. Bat cocked and at the ready, he stepped into the room.

There was no one there.

His breathing and heartrate began to slow considerably, as the odds that anyone had broken in were becoming less and less likely. Just the same, Oliver remained guarded, and methodically checked the rest of the house.

It was a little after midnight.

Once certain no one was inside the house, he turned on the

outside lights, including the floodlights that illuminated the backyard. The area was barren and empty, all the lawn furniture put away
for the winter. The shed near the rear of the property appeared un-
disturbed, as did the stockade fence enclosing it.

Craning his neck, he checked the bulkhead door leading to the
cellar, which was located outside near the corner of the house. The
lock was in place, the iron door intact.

Oliver let out a sigh that was equal parts relief and exhaustion,
and then leaned against the counter to collect his thoughts. Emily was understandably on edge. Maybe she'd mistaken an everyday
noise for something far more sinister and became spooked, fearful
as she'd been earlier that the man in the fedora had somehow found
them.

"I swore I heard someone down here."

"Jesus!" Startled, Oliver spun toward the sound of her voice.
"Emily, you scared the shit out of me." He put a hand to his chest.
"I didn't hear you come down the stairs."

"I was trying to be quiet."

"There's no one here but us."

"Did you look in the basement?" she asked, the harried emotion
that had dominated her tone previously suddenly absent now.

"No," he said, leaning the baseball bat in the corner. "Only way
in is through the bulkhead outside. Padlock's in place, no one got
into the cellar."

"You're sure?"

"Emily, I promise you."

"Okay." She hugged herself and nodded, looking away. "Sorry."

"Don't be. It's always better to be safe."

"Safe," she said breathlessly, like it was possibly the most ridiculous word she'd ever heard.

Now clad in a tight white tank top t-shirt and a pair of light blue
flannel pajama pants, Oliver realized Emily had taken her bathrobe
off at some point before coming downstairs.

He also realized there was something terribly wrong.

"Emily," he said, his heart again racing as he focused on a large
stain developing along the side of her tank top, a bright red blossom
soaking through the thin white material. "You're—Emily—you're
bleeding."

She glanced down at the stain. "I thought it stopped. They keep opening up again. It's not as bad as it looks, they…they just won't stop bleeding."

"What happened?" He remembered the bathwater. "Did you hurt yourself in the tub?"

Emily touched the wetness, her fingertips coming back slick with crimson. Rubbing them together, she gazed at her fingers as if she'd never seen blood before. "The wounds," she said, like Oliver should know perfectly well what she was referring to, "they keep opening."

"*Wounds?*" he said, moving toward her cautiously. "What *wounds?*"

"They only bleed for a few minutes."

"Sweetie, what the hell are you talking about?"

"It stops, but then they open up again. It'll stop soon, you'll see. Maybe this time it won't start up again." Emily raised the side of her top up to just below her breasts. Fresh blood, slick and bright, covered her side from her hip bone to ribcage. "That's where he did it," she said, eyes dull and distant, her voice flat, robotic.

"Jesus Christ." Oliver snatched a roll of paper towels from the holder on the counter and quickly tore off several sheets. Before he could place it against her side, Emily took them from him and did it herself. "What is going on?" he asked frantically, his head spinning. "How did you—"

"Oliver, I just told you. That's where he did it."

"That's where *who* did *what?*"

"The man in the fedora," she said.

As his heart sunk and a clammy layer of perspiration rapidly coated his entire body, Oliver shook his head, as if this might somehow help him better understand and manage the terror coursing through him. "The man…"

"The man in the fedora," she said again, pointing to her side. "That's where he did it."

Oliver forced a swallow. "That's where he did *what*, Emily?"

She didn't answer right away, but when she did, it was with the same dead eyes and monotone voice she'd acquired since finding him in the kitchen.

"That's where he bit me."

6

The den was small and somewhat cramped. Cluttered with knick-knacks—colorful paperweights, commemorative plates and little fig-urines everywhere—the room had the feel of a quaint New England gift shop rather than a space where people actually lived and spent time. An enormous grandfather clock stood in the corner, ticking softly, the pendulum swaying behind a slim door of etched glass. A brass lamp with an ornate ceramic shade provided the only light, cast-ing the small room in a soft and strange orange glow.

Sitting forward in a comfortable chair, Oliver waited, hands in his lap.

In her bathrobe and slippers, Maureen Adelson sat across from him on a plush couch, looking at once concerned and perplexed. Sans makeup, and her snow-white hair brushed straight back from her face in a rather severe manner, she also looked much older and disheveled than the normally well-groomed and meticulously coiffed woman Oliver had become accustomed to over the years.

For some time, the only sound in the room was the ticking of the clock.

"Are you sure I can't get you anything?" Maureen asked.

"Thank you, no, I'm fine. We've been enough of an inconvenience."

"Don't be silly." She smiled awkwardly then looked away.

"I'm so sorry to have bothered you and Ezra at this hour, I—"

"It's fine, really," Maureen insisted. "I'm just glad Ezra could help."

Oliver stole a quick peek at the grandfather clock. 1:33.

At the end of a hall just off the den, a door creaked open then closed. A moment later Ezra Adelson entered the room, a cross look on his craggy face and a small terrycloth towel in his hands, which he was still using to wipe them off. "She's fine," he said in his typical gravelly baritone. Clad in a bathrobe, a set of flannel pajamas beneath, and a pair of scuffed leather slippers on his feet, his thick silver hair was combed perfectly despite the late hour, and with his hound dog eyes and jowls, Ezra Adelson looked like a country doctor straight out of a classic black-and-white film. "She'll be out in a minute."

"It's nothing too serious then?" Oliver asked.

"Would you excuse us, please, dear?" Ezra said, giving his wife the eye.

"Of course," Maureen said, pushing herself back to her feet.

"Why don't you go on back to bed?" Ezra told her. "I'll be right up."

"I'm glad everything's all right with Emily," Maureen said, smiling. "Give her my best. Goodnight, Oliver."

"Goodnight," Oliver said sheepishly.

Ezra waited until his wife had climbed the creaky stairs to their bedroom before he threw the towel over his shoulder and said, "I cleaned and dressed the wounds, and while they don't appear to be infected, I wrote Emily a prescription for a round of antibiotics just to be safe. The bleeding has stopped and I don't expect it to start again. Long as she takes the antibiotics and keeps the affected area clean and dry, and takes it easy with any activities that might strain her abdomen for a while, she should be fine. Her wounds are in a precarious location but weren't terribly deep and don't appear to be infected, as I said, so I don't anticipate any serious issues. However, she should follow up with her regular physician, do you understand?"

"Yes, of course."

Ezra nodded, deeming his response acceptable. "Oliver, you put me in one hell of a position here tonight."

"I'm sorry to have bothered you with this so late, Ezra, I really am, I—"

"I don't practice at home. In fact, I'm semi-retired and barely practice at all these days. You should've taken your wife to the ER."

"I wanted to, but she wouldn't go. I had a hell of a time getting her over here to see you, let alone—"

"Well it's no wonder," Ezra said, shaking his head. "After seeing Emily's abdomen, it's no wonder at all."

"I wanted to take her, Ezra. She refused."

"So instead of calling an ambulance or insisting she go, you walk her over here and pound on our door at one o'clock in the morning?"

"I'm sorry about the late hour, I—"

"There are laws," he said, hands on his hips. "Laws and procedures, Oliver, and if I don't follow them I'm committing a criminal act."

Oliver sat looking up at Ezra, thoroughly confused. "I don't understand."

"I could lose my license. Do you understand *that?*"

"What have I done to jeopardize your license?"

"Things of this nature have to be reported today."

"Of *what* nature, what do you mean?"

He watched Oliver a while, clearly weighing the validity of his question. "You saw Emily's wounds, yes?"

"Not exactly," Oliver said. "I saw blood on her side, but I couldn't make out the actual wounds."

Ezra frowned. "And how do you suppose she get those wounds, Oliver?"

"I don't know."

"You don't know."

"No, I don't." Oliver remembered telling Emily to simply tell Ezra that something had bitten her, but not to mention the man in the fedora or anything that had happened earlier that night. Now he couldn't be sure what she'd told him. "She told me something bit her."

We'll just go to Ezra's and let him check you out, all right?

"And you have no idea what that something might've been?"

I don't want to go outside. What if he's out there waiting for us?

"I saw that she was bleeding and needed medical attention. I tried to convince her to let me take her to the hospital, but she refused. Finally, I was able to convince her to walk over here with me and let you take a look at her."

There's no one out there, Emily, I promise you, there's no one out there.

Snow began to fall, the flakes dancing in darkness beyond the window.

"There are two puncture wounds, about four inches apart, on the side of her abdomen," Ezra explained. "They're aligned perfectly and quite symmetrical. Luckily, as I mentioned, they're not terribly deep.

Had they been any deeper the result would've been a far more serious injury."

"So what caused them?"

"I'm not a forensic specialist by any stretch of the imagination," Ezra sighed, "but I can tell you this. I saw nothing that would indicate the wounds Emily sustained were caused by a bite from an animal, and they certainly weren't from a human being."

"Then how did she get them?"

"You don't have any idea?"

"I didn't even realize she was hurt. Did you ask her? What did she say?"

"She told me she thought something bit her. When I asked what, she said she had no idea, and that she didn't realize the wounds were even there until they began to bleed."

"Is that possible?"

"If you're asking me if I believe her, no, I do not." Ezra moved to the lone window in the room, which faced the street, and gazed out into the night. "And I haven't even gotten to the alcohol yet. You've both been drinking."

"We went to a party earlier, had a few drinks, nothing excessive."

Ezra sighed heavily. "You honestly don't know how Emily sustained those wounds? Is that what you're telling me?"

"That's exactly what I'm telling you, yes."

"My guess is that the punctures on Emily's abdomen were caused by a large cooking fork, or something similar."

Oliver slowly rose to his feet. "What?"

"Emily wasn't bitten by anything." Ezra turned away from the window and faced Oliver again. "She was stabbed."

His mind raced for answers. "I…I don't—"

"Did you two have an argument?"

"No, nothing like that, everything's fine."

"Has Emily been having any difficulties lately, emotional or mental?"

"Not that I'm aware of, no."

"She seemed a bit removed. *Absent*, you might say, when I was examining and speaking with her. She didn't seem herself."

Oliver ran a hand through his closely cropped hair. "Ezra, are you suggesting the wounds were self-inflicted?"

"I'm not suggesting anything. But you and I both know there are only a few possibilities here. Either someone stabbed Emily, or she stabbed herself. Is there something more you want to tell me about this?"

"I didn't assault my wife with a cooking fork or anything else."

"Did someone else?"

"I don't see how that's possible."

"Perhaps it was an accident then, yes?" Ezra tightened the belt on his robe and arched a bushy gray eyebrow. "Look, it's the middle of the goddamn night. I'm an old man and I'm tired. Against my better judgment, I'm going to let this go for now. But listen to me very carefully. Should this ever become an issue beyond the three of us, my explanation will be that it was an accident. I'll say that's how you two presented it to me, that Emily *accidentally* stabbed herself with a cooking fork. She lost her balance while carrying it, fell into it, and was injured. Unsure of the extent of her injuries, rather than call an ambulance you brought her here and I examined her, cleaned the wounds and wrote her a prescription. It was a simple domestic *accident*. They happen all the time. Do we understand each other?"

Oliver nodded. "Yes."

"I strongly suggest you two seek professional help. Whatever really took place tonight, it could've been far worse. Next time Emily might not be so lucky."

"Thank you." Oliver offered his hand.

Ezra stared at him with his intense but droopy eyes.

"You don't honestly think I had anything to do with this, do you?" Oliver smiled nervously. "I'd never hurt Emily. You know me better than that, Ezra. For God's sake, we've been friends for years."

"We've been *neighbors* for years." Ezra folded his arms across his chest. "We're not friends, Oliver. I barely know you."

The door at the end of the hall opened, and Oliver heard Emily's footfalls slowly approaching. He dropped his hand to his side. "Thanks for your help."

"You're welcome," the old man said. "Now if you don't mind, I'd like to get back to sleep. So please, do us both a favor. Take your wife and get the hell out of my house."

7

The memories of rushing hand-in-hand with Emily through the darkness were still fresh in Oliver's mind. They'd made it home in record time, Emily's head on a swivel the entire time, as she whispered about the man in the fedora.

Once back in the alleged safety of their kitchen, Emily ferociously chugged orange juice straight from the carton. It ran down her chin and across the front of her, but she seemed to neither care nor even notice. Finished, she returned the carton to the refrigerator then wiped her mouth with the back of her hand.

Oliver grabbed one of the towels hanging from the stove and handed it to her. "Clean yourself up."

She stared at him as if she hadn't understood.

"There's orange juice all down the front of you."

Emily glanced down at her chest, saw the mess, then reached out and took the towel from him. "Sorry."

"How did you get those wounds, Emily?"

"I already told you," she said softly, wiping off her tank top.

"We never stopped, and the man didn't follow us, so it's not possible he—"

"Are you sure?"

"Other than clipping him with the car we had no interaction with the man."

Satisfied with the state of her tank top, Emily carefully folded the towel then hung it back over the oven handle.

"Did you hear what I said?" Oliver pressed.

"I heard you, Oliver. I'm not deaf."

"Whatever happened to you, that old man in the fedora had nothing to do with it. Now I know it's been a long and stressful night, and you've been through a lot, but I need you to tell me what the hell is going on. Right now, Emily." When she offered nothing more, Oliver said, "Ezra told me the wounds weren't bites. He said they were caused by some sort of utensil, likely a cooking fork."

"He's wrong."

"Ezra said they were quite possibly self-inflicted, Emily."

"Why do you care what that dirty old fool says?"

"*Dirty old fool?*"

Emily moved closer. "Did you know he made me take all my clothes off?"

"Well, he—I mean—he's a doctor, sweetheart, there must've been a good reason. He probably needed to get a close look at the wounds without—"

"Then why did he make me take my bottoms off too?"

Oliver shook his head. The exhaustion was winning and he felt like he was losing whatever shred of his sanity he had left. "I don't know, I—what are you saying? Did Ezra do something inappropriate?"

She gave a devilish grin. "He gave me a *very* thorough exam, Oliver."

"You shouldn't joke about things like that. Ezra's a good man."

"Who said I was joking?"

"This isn't funny, Emily."

"You should've seen it from my end."

"What the hell does that mean?"

"What do you think it means?" Emily cupped her breasts, pushed them together and began bouncing them with her hands. The tank top left very little to the imagination, and her nipples were suddenly very hard and straining against the thin material. "You like that?"

"What the hell are you doing?"

She let herself go. "When did you become so boring? *Such* a pussy."

"What is the matter with you?"

"What's the matter with *you?* Where's the man I married?"

"I'm right here."

"No, he's been replaced with a whiny little faggot."

"Since when do you use that word?"

"What are you, the word police?"

"Emily—"

"Oh, fuck off." She wandered over to the doorway, suddenly appearing as if she might nod off to sleep at any second. "I need to...I need to go to bed."

"I know it's late but I think I ought to take you over to the hospital. You're not yourself."

"I'm just tired. I'm not going anywhere but upstairs to bed."

Unsure of how to handle her erratic behavior, and not wanting to escalate things further, Oliver followed her upstairs without further argument.

After he'd gotten her a fresh top to sleep in and tossed the tank top with the bloodstains in the hamper, Emily crawled into bed, lay back and pulled the covers up tight to her chin, the way a child might.

"I'm sorry about before, I..."

"It's all right. We'll talk in the morning."

"Can you stay downstairs tonight?" she asked. "Keep watch?"

There seemed little point in arguing with her. "Okay," he said. "Get some rest. Goodnight."

"Goodnight."

Oliver changed into a pair of pajama bottoms and a sweatshirt, then bent over and kissed her forehead, but Emily was already asleep and snoring softly. He whispered, "I love you," then slipped into the master bathroom and closed the door behind him. After brushing his teeth he checked the bathroom for any clues or signs as to what Emily might've used to inflict the wounds on her abdomen.

There was nothing in the medicine cabinet or beneath the sink, nothing in the wastebasket that could've caused them. The bathtub was empty, but the sides were still stained with swathes of blood, the water having left them a light pink color.

Oliver checked the closet. Nothing but linens, towels, a makeup mirror and a few cleaning supplies. Could she have taken something from the kitchen then returned it without him knowing? Possible, but why do such a thing?

Nothing made sense anymore.

That's where he bit me.

The party seemed so long ago now.

Oliver switched off the light then moved into the hallway, pulling the door closed behind him.

Back downstairs, he checked the trash but found nothing, so he tried the various drawers that housed their cooking utensils. They had a couple large cooking forks, one designed for indoor use and another for the backyard grill, but both were in the drawer, the prongs clean.

Oliver settled on the couch and tried to calm his nerves. Stretching out, he put his head on a pillow and drew a deep breath. The light was scarce but it didn't matter. Spending the night downstairs probably wasn't a bad idea after all, because exhausted as he was, Oliver was sure he wouldn't get much sleep anyway. In fact, he was certain he wouldn't sleep again for quite some time, which is why he had no idea that the moment he closed his eyes he would immediately spiral down into a netherworld of darkness and dreams.

Lost in the night…blind, deaf and unable to call out for help, he shivered with fear. From the shadowy corners of his dead eyes, an old man in a fedora watched and waited, laughing quietly.

It was the most terrifying sound Oliver had ever heard.

8

He awakened to a cold and empty house.

Oliver stood in the kitchen, gripping a mug of steaming coffee, the heat welcome and warming in his hands. Still a bit groggy from what had been an unexpectedly deep sleep, he found himself alone in the house, the SUV missing from the driveway. His watch read: 9:12. It wasn't like Emily to leave the house this early on a weekend, and completely out-of-character for her to do so without leaving a note to let him know where she'd gone. But there was no note, and no Emily, and although given the way she'd been acting it didn't exactly surprise him, it was troubling nonetheless. The last thing Oliver needed was to worry about his wife wandering around in public behaving as peculiarly as she had the night before.

As he drifted into the living room, coffee in one hand and his cell in the other, he selected Emily's number from his contact list then stood before the windows as the call connected.

The day was overcast and foggy, the dark gray skies threatening rain or perhaps even more snow. But what caught Oliver's attention was the unmarked black sedan parked in front of Ezra's house, and the heavyset woman standing with Ezra at the foot of his driveway. They stood close to each other and seemed to be discussing something very intently, occasionally glancing in the direction of his house as they did so. At one point they seemed to look right at him, so Oliver stepped away from the windows, hoping they hadn't seen him.

If the woman's rigid demeanor, nondescript black pantsuit and sensible shoes hadn't given her away—and they had—the car certainly did. No one drove cars that looked like that except the police.

"This is Emily," his wife's voice suddenly said in his ear, "leave a message and I'll get back soon as I can. Thanks!"

After the tone, Oliver said, "Where are you? I'm worried, didn't know you were going anywhere this morning. Give me a call soon as you get this, okay?"

Oliver disconnected the phone and returned to the windows.

Ezra, in the same bathrobe and pajamas he'd been wearing the night before, continued to talk with the woman, but they seemed more focused on each other now. In the meantime, his other neighbor, Stan Gill, or simply *Gilly* as he liked to be called, had emerged from his house and taken up position on the border between his and Oliver's yard. He watched Ezra and the cop intently, arms folded across his chest and a disapproving look on his face.

Tucking his phone into his pajama pocket, Oliver made his way back into the kitchen and out the front door. The cold air hit him like a slap to the face. He immediately regretted not changing clothes before venturing outside, but remained on the stone walkway, sipping his coffee and feigning indifference.

Fog drifted around him like ghosts.

Having seen him, Gilly cocked his shaved head toward the others, rolled his eyes then sauntered over to Oliver. "Get a load of this one," he said. "That's what passes for a cop these days apparently."

Although he'd known him for a few years, Oliver was never clear on exactly what Gilly had done for a living. He only knew he'd been some sort of bigshot organizer in a construction worker's union in Boston, and tended to be something of a conspiracy nut who behaved in a paranoid manner, as if he was under constant surveillance. Ironic, since Gilly missed virtually nothing in the neighborhood himself. A short man with an often aggressive and crude manner Oliver didn't much care for, Gilly was nonetheless a good neighbor, and usually nice to him and Emily, even though they had little in common. His wife Melinda (who they learned not long after meeting her was Gilly's second wife) was thirty years his junior, didn't work and was never up and about at this hour.

"What's going on?" Oliver asked.

"No idea, but she's been over there talking to Adelson for a while." Gilly dropped his hands to his hips. "Always got a wild root growing up his ass, that one. You know he's still giving me crap about the spotlight in my front yard? Shouldn't be motion-tripped, he says. Comes on every time a squirrel crosses my yard, he says, shines in his bedroom windows, wakes him and his wife up at all hours, he says. What the hell good would it be if it's not motion-tripped? I'd have to leave it on all night if it wasn't, then he'd bitch about that. Jackass, look at him all cozy and whispering with her over there."

"What do you think she wants?"

"I'm guessing it's not a salad."

"Jesus, Stan."

"Oh come on, look at her. Must be at least fifty pounds overweight and pushing sixty, couldn't run a city block with a gun to her head. But, you know, she's a broad, so let's give her the job anyway so we can all feel like we did something meaningful."

"Stop," Oliver said. "Please, not today, all right? Just *stop*."

"Relax, PC Polly." Gilly held his hands up like the victim of a robbery. "Just two guys talking, am I right?"

Ignoring him, Oliver drifted a few steps away. Sipping his coffee and attempting to appear as nonchalant as possible, he watched as the woman said something more to Ezra then began walking across the road toward them. Ambling through the heavy fog, she looked almost ethereal.

"And look, she's a detective no less," Gilly chuckled.

Oliver's heart began to race. "How do you know she's a detective?"

"Look at her waist, or where her waist is supposed to be."

Attached to the woman's belt was a gold shield, mostly obscured by her jacket. Oliver hadn't noticed it, but once he had he couldn't take his eyes off it. What was a detective doing in their neighborhood? Until that moment, Oliver hadn't realized the police department in town even had detectives.

Before Oliver could think any more about it, the woman had moved up the pathway to his front door. "Mr. Young?" she asked while still several feet away.

"Yes," Oliver said, hoping he hadn't sounded nearly as nervous as he felt.

Gilly widened his stance but said nothing.

"I'm Detective Joan Brenda." She held her jacket open to show the badge then let it go and extended her hand. "Good morning."

"Good morning." Oliver shook her hand. Hers was a firm grip, her palm soft and warm. "Oliver Young."

Detective Brenda shifted her dark eyes to Gilly and gave a slight nod in his direction. "Good morning, Mr. Gill."

He arched an eyebrow. "How do you know my name?"

"Well now, how do you suppose? I am the police, after all." She smiled, very slowly. "It's a matter of public record, nothing nefarious, hate to disappoint."

"So what's this all about then, Ms. Brenda?" Gilly asked with a smirk.

"*Detective* Brenda," she corrected him.

"I'll bet that makes you feel mighty important, doesn't it?"

The detective considered him a bit longer than necessary, as if she'd planned a response, but instead turned to Oliver and said, "Mr. Young, I'd like to speak with you privately if I might."

"Is there something wrong?" Oliver asked.

"I just have some routine questions, if you wouldn't mind."

Oliver felt a smile twitch across his lips. "Questions regarding…"

"Again, I'd prefer to speak privately, if you don't mind."

"Not at all," Oliver said, motioning to his front door. "Please, come in."

"Be next door if you need me," Gilly said, drifting back toward his house.

Oliver ushered Detective Brenda inside, closed the door behind them then led her deeper into the kitchen. "Sorry about Stan," he said, clearing his throat. "He has some issues with authority."

"If we all spent time apologizing for the behavior of our neighbors these days, I suspect we wouldn't have time for much else."

"To be honest, I don't really know him that well."

"Oh, he's not that complicated. I think we both know enough, don't you?"

Oliver felt himself blush but forced a smile and nodded. "Can I offer you a cup of coffee, Detective Brenda?"

"Already had two," she said, glancing around. "Doctor says that ought to be the limit, so I'm doing my best to listen. But thank you kindly."

Oliver pushed a pile of mail to the other side of the kitchen table. "I'm sorry about the mess. Please, have a seat."

Detective Brenda dropped into a chair facing him. "Have you and Mrs. Young been away?"

"I'm sorry?"

"That's an awful lot of unopened mail you've got there."

Oliver felt his stomach clench. "Yes," he said, smiling nervously. "I mean, no, we—we haven't been away. I'm behind in going through the mail, that's all. We get a lot of mail for some reason and it tends to pile up if I don't sort through it right away."

"I see." The detective watched him a moment. "There's no need to be nervous, Mr. Young. I just need to ask you a few questions."

"I'm not nervous," Oliver assured her, but the moment the words left his mouth he wished they hadn't. "Well, maybe a little. It's just—well—I'm not used to being questioned by the police."

"Good to hear." She pulled a pen and small pad from the inside pocket of her jacket then adjusted her position. She seemed to be having trouble getting comfortable and situated in the chair, as if she were dealing with some sort of physical pain. "People who are tend to be criminals."

Oliver gave an obligatory smile then sat down in the chair across from her. "How can I help you?"

"Is Mrs. Young at home?" she asked, glancing around again. Her dark hair, specked with gray and combed straight back from her face in a rather severe manner, was braided at the ends and adorned with multi-colored beads that made a soft clicking sound whenever she moved her head.

"She's out at the moment."

Detective Brenda reached for a pair of eyeglasses hanging from a chain around her neck and slid them on. "When do you expect her?"

"I'm not sure. She went to do some grocery shopping."

It disturbed Oliver how easily he'd begun to lie. He'd never been like this before, and yet now he couldn't stop, even though it had already gone too far. But what exactly, *what* had gone too far? What was happening to him? What was happening to *them*?

"Can you tell me what this is all about, detective?"

"There was an incident in town last night."

When she offered nothing more Oliver said, "An incident?"

"A hit-and-run over on Main Street."

57

Oliver held her gaze, doing everything in his power to remain calm, but it felt like his entire body had begun to quake uncontrollably. "Hopefully no one was seriously hurt," he managed.

"Regardless," she said, "it's still a very serious crime."

"What does any of this have to do with me?"

"According to the victim, the driver's car was very similar to your Impala."

Oliver wanted to say something, anything, but he couldn't find the words and instead sat there stupidly, smiling at her.

"While the victim couldn't be certain of the make," Detective Brenda continued, "it's the same size, color and general description."

"Huh. Well, it is a fairly common looking car."

"Be that as it may, we're obligated to check into it. As a matter of procedure, you understand."

"Certainly, but I can tell you we had nothing to with anything like that."

"That's why I'm here." She glanced up at him over her reading glasses. "To clear things up, so there aren't any misunderstandings."

"How can I help you then?"

"Can you tell me your whereabouts last evening, please?"

"My wife and I were at a party at a friend's house."

"Here in town?"

"Yes."

She jotted something down on her pad. "And what time was the party?"

"I believe we got there around seven or so."

"Do you remember what time you and Mrs. Young left the party?"

Oliver pretended to think about it. "Around ten, I think."

"When you say you *think* do you mean you're not sure?"

"I'm relatively sure it was around ten."

"And when did you arrive at home?"

"Just a few minutes later, the party was over on Elmwood Way."

Detective Brenda looked up from her pad. "So you would've taken Main Street on your way home then?"

"Yeah, we—yes—we did."

"Were you and Mrs. Young drinking at the party?"

"We had a couple cocktails."

"As in two? Or would you say more than that?"

"We weren't intoxicated if that's what you're asking."

"Were you driving, Mr. Young?"

"My wife drove us home."

"And you took the Impala that's parked in your driveway, is that correct?"

"That's correct." Despite the chill in the house, Oliver's palms began to sweat. He casually wiped them on his pajama pants.

"Can you tell me the names of the friends who threw the party?"

"Is that really necessary?"

"Is there some reason you'd rather not give me their names?"

"I guess I just don't see the point in involving or bothering them with this."

"Well, if they verify your whereabouts last night and confirm the times you arrived and left—as I'm sure they can—that would be extremely helpful."

Before Oliver could stop it, a burst of nervous laughter escaped him. He clutched his mug of coffee in the hopes it would mask the shaking in his hands. "Do you—I mean—I certainly hope we're not *suspects* in this. We had nothing to do with any hit-and-run. In all fairness, a lot of people have silver sedans these days, and if my wife and I ever hit someone with our car we'd never in a million years keep driving, we'd stop to make sure they were all right. We're law-abiding citizens, we—I—I can't even remember the last time either of us even had a parking or speeding ticket, I—"

"Mr. Young, relax, no one's accusing you or your wife of anything."

Oliver realized then he'd been talking very quickly. He drew a deep breath, sat back a bit in his chair and sipped his coffee. "I certainly hope not."

As Detective Brenda sat forward, her jacket fell open to reveal a cream colored sweater, her gold shield, and the butt of a holstered 9mm under her left arm. "I know this sort of thing can be off-putting to someone not accustomed to dealing with the police," she told him, "but I need to go through the motions, cross the t's and dot the i's, as it were. I'm just doing my job, Mr. Young."

"Sure, I understand."

"Then, if you wouldn't mind, what are the names of your friends?"

"William and Nora McClure."

"And the McClures' address?"

"Seven Elmwood Way."

Detective Brenda wrote it down in her pad. "I'll be sure to use the utmost discretion when approaching them, Mr. Young."

"Thank you, I'd appreciate it."

She smiled in what seemed a warm and genuine manner for the first time. "Well, I thank you for your cooperation."

"I hope you find the person responsible for this."

She looked at him. "Oh, I will."

A spasm-like smile danced along Oliver's lips.

"I was speaking with Doctor Adelson earlier," she said. "He mentioned you and your wife did have some difficulty last night."

Oliver remained still, his mind racing almost as fast as his heart. "Can I ask why you were discussing us with Ezra?"

"I've known Doc Adelson for a while," she said. "I was just saying hello, explaining I was coming to speak with you when he mentioned it."

"I'm not really sure that's appropriate, but—"

"Something about a cooking fork, he said."

"Yes, an accident."

"An accident?" the detective arched an eyebrow.

"My wife tripped and stabbed herself with the damn thing."

"Ouch."

"Luckily Ezra was able to treat her. It wasn't too bad."

"Sounds like it could've been much worse, glad to hear she's all right."

Oliver nodded but said nothing more.

"Speaking of your wife," Detective Brenda said, closing her pad, "I'd like to speak with her as well at some point."

"Why's that?"

"Would you rather I not?"

Oliver smiled so hard his jaw hurt. "I have no issue with you speaking to her, ma'am," he said. "I just don't understand why it's necessary."

"Is your wife coming back, Mr. Young?" she asked evenly.

"She lives here, I sure hope so." Oliver laughed lightly, but upon seeing Detective Brenda's humorless expression added, "Yes, of course she is. Why wouldn't she be?"

"I'll leave you my card then. Ask Mrs. Young to give me a call at her earliest convenience. If you'll notice, I've crossed out the original number and jotted down a new one. Have her call that one, please. My direct number changed and, well, with budget cuts and all, they haven't printed us up new cards yet, so…"

Oliver watched as the detective took a business card from her jacket pocket and handed it to him. Steadying his hand best he could, he took it, glanced at it quickly then placed it on the table.

"Or, if she'd rather, I can come back and speak with her at another time."

"I'll be sure she gets the message."

"Thank you, Mr. Young." Detective Brenda rose to her feet and hitched her pants up awkwardly. "That's quite a bump you've got there."

"What do you mean?"

"Above your eye," she said, pointing. "Nice little egg there."

Oliver touched his forehead. His fingers found a lump about the size of a small marble. He hadn't realized when his head hit the window it had left a mark, but it had apparently swollen overnight, and now hurt to the touch. He winced reflexively. "It's nothing, really."

"From the looks, must've hit your head awfully hard."

"I wasn't watching where I was going for a change," he said, forcing a laugh. "Walked right into a door, I'm graceful that way. Still hurts a little."

"I bet. Sounds like you and your wife had all sorts of accidents last night."

"Oh no, this was from a couple days ago, actually."

She stared at him but gave no response. The feel of her stare subtly told him she was looking, maybe even hoping, for something more from him. It was almost as if she was waiting for some form of recognition.

"Is there anything else?" Oliver asked.

"No, I suppose that's all for now, Mr. Young. Thank you for your time, and I'm sorry to have bothered you on a Saturday morning."

"No bother, just wish I could be of more help." Oliver walked her to the door. "Have a good weekend."

"You do the same," she said, slipping outside. Turning back, she looked him up and down again, this time without subtly. "Take good care now."

Once she was outside and Oliver had closed the door, he hurried over to the windows and watched as the detective casually inspected the front and passenger side of the Impala. Apparently satisfied with what she'd seen—or perhaps with what she hadn't—she started back down the driveway to her car across the street. As she turned, her jacket fell open, and though she quickly pulled it closed, Oliver knew he'd seen something he hadn't before.

A stain, seeping through her sweater, just above her gold shield…

Oliver trembled. The world crashed around him like walls collapsing from every direction, drowning him in madness, crushing, suffocating him.

…a slowly growing crimson blossom…

Lost in terror the likes of which he'd never known, his throat constricted, strangling him, and he began to gag.

…Detective Brenda was bleeding…

Just like Emily.

9

The fog remained, joined by heavy winds. Under a gray and dreary sky, a line of barren trees along the far side of the pond swayed against the onslaught, leaves and other debris along the ground dancing about and riding the surges as the temperature continued to plummet.

But for Oliver and Will, who sat huddled on a bench between a bike path and the pond, and a lone young woman walking along the far banks, the park was empty. They'd sat in silence so long Oliver wondered if Will planned on responding, and now began to question his judgment in having confided in him in the first place.

Finally, Will said, "Okay." Then he sighed, his breath tumbling free in a burst of cloud-like smoke as it hit the frigid air. "You've given me a lot to deal with here."

Oliver stuffed his hands deeper into the pockets of his coat and tucked chin to chest as the wind picked up again, cutting through them like razors. "Everything's wrong, Will. Nothing makes sense, and it's getting worse."

"You guys really should've stopped."

"After everything that's happened, I'm glad we didn't."

Will stretched his long legs out, away from the bench. "We felt really bad about what happened at the party." He pushed his wire-framed eyeglasses a bit higher on his narrow nose. "Now I can't help but think it contributed to all this. If you guys hadn't left when you did, maybe none of this would've happened."

"But we did leave, and it did happen."

"Which is why you should probably be lawyering up instead of sitting here talking to me," Will told him. "That said, I'm sorry, but I have to ask. Exactly *how* did Emily get those wounds?"

"I have no idea." Oliver wished he'd worn a hat. His ears were freezing, and every time the wind whipped past they stung. "Like I said, she told me the man *bit* her, of all things, but Ezra said it was some sort of fork or something."

Will, who until then had been gazing out at the frozen pond, slowly turned and looked at him. "Did she stab herself?"

"I don't know," Oliver said desperately.

"The guy she hit, did—"

"She just clipped him, it's not like we ran him down."

"Okay, but you said she never completely stopped the car, right?"

"That's right." Oliver rubbed his ears, trying to warm them. "I don't think we ever actually stopped."

"You don't *think* you did, or you didn't?"

"I don't know, I—I'm relatively sure we didn't."

"This is kind of an important point, pal. How could you not know?"

"I don't have any memory of the car ever coming to a complete stop, but the whole thing is sort of hazy, almost like a dream, you know?"

"So whether you stopped for a second or two or didn't, whatever, neither of you ever left the car, right?"

Visions of the man in the fedora, his unfinished face drifting past the car window, flashed in Oliver's mind. "No," he answered, but couldn't truly be sure.

"And the man never got *into* the car?"

"Of course not," Oliver said. Why couldn't he be certain?

"Then we can rule him out as being the culprit, which means Ezra's right. Emily wasn't bitten, she was stabbed. So how did that happen?"

"Will, I'm telling you, *I don't know.*"

"Well, unless Emily's suddenly started to show signs of stigmata, I'd say we can conclude her wounds didn't miraculously appear from nowhere."

Oliver looked out at the pond. The woman was still on the other side, her back to them now as she faced the trees. He focused on the knit hat she wore, and the pink pompom on top. It looked nice and warm. "There's something happening, Will, something bad. The man in the fedora, there was something wrong about him."

"I don't follow, wrong how?"

"I don't know." Oliver clamped shut his eyes. Visions of the man in the fedora sprung out at him from the dark like a funhouse jump-scare. He quickly opened his eyes and tried to focus instead on the pond. "I'm just not sure Emily and I remember everything about that night correctly. It should've only taken us a few minutes to get home from your place, but when we walked in the door, I looked at the clock. Almost an hour had gone by."

Will frowned. "Losing time, confusion, all these things you're telling me, could easily be caused from hitting your heads, you do realize that, right?"

"Emily never hit her head. Ezra said nothing about that either, her having a concussion or anything similar. Except for the wounds, he said she was fine."

"*She* was fine," Will said.

"You think this is all me? What, like I've lost my mind?"

"I didn't say that. Did I say that?"

"Emily's the one who hasn't been herself since the accident. There were times last night she was like a completely different person, Will. I'm not even sure where she is right now. I'm hoping she went out to fill the prescription Ezra wrote for her, but who knows? She was already gone when I got up and she's not answering her phone. That's not Emily. There's something more going on."

"You keep saying that but you're not telling me what."

"Because I don't know," Oliver insisted. "How did the police get to us so quickly? Even if the guy went straight home and reported the incident, how did a detective find our car and come to question us not even twenty-four hours after the whole thing happened?"

"That does seem awfully fast, I'll grant you that. But it doesn't mean—"

"Besides, we're far from the only ones with a silver sedan in town or even a silver or gray Impala. That cop acted like she already knew we did it, like she was playing along for some reason."

"Cops act like that sometimes. It doesn't always mean anything."

"True, but at one point, I would've sworn she *knew* me, recognized me, Will, and was waiting for me to do the same."

"Maybe you met at some point."

"No, I've never seen her before. And what about *her* wound, what are the odds that she'd have a wound like that in the same part of her body Emily does?"

"You're sure that couldn't have been something else? You said yourself she was across the street at the time, maybe—"

"I know what I saw, Will. There was a bloodstain on her sweater."

"But you didn't see it when she was in your kitchen?"

"No, I either didn't notice it or her jacket was covering it. Maybe, like Emily's, it only bleeds periodically and it didn't start up until she went outside."

"Could it have been a food or drink stain, maybe, or—"

"You're not hearing me, man. It was in the same spot Emily was bleeding from, the exact same spot."

"Okay," Will said, obviously treading carefully, "but wouldn't that also be a common spot on the body where someone might spill something?"

"It was blood. The stain was growing, just like Emily's. She was *bleeding*, Will, from the abdomen, the same as Emily was last night."

His lanky body stretched out and leaned back against the bench, and his sandy brown hair, which he wore a bit long, blew around in the wind. Will seemed to think about this a while before responding. "When you went to Ezra's, did he check you out at all?"

"No, I was fine, I—I *am* fine, I'm telling you this isn't about me, it's—"

"And the bump on your head?"

"It's nothing."

"I don't know if I'd say it's *nothing*, Oliver."

"You're not listening to me, you—"

"I *am* listening. You're not exactly making a whole lot of sense here." Will's cheeks flushed red in the cold. "Look, I'm doing my best, all right? You hit your head on the window pretty hard, so getting it checked out probably isn't the worst idea, that's all I'm saying. You shouldn't take chances when it comes to a head injury."

"I don't have a *head injury*," Oliver said, watching the woman across the pond again. She'd moved closer to the trees, her back still to them and her arms at her side. She seemed to be watching the tree line intently but he couldn't make anything out beyond or between the trees, so it was unclear what she was either looking at or for. But she stood perfectly still, as if mesmerized. "It's just a little bump."

"You can never be too careful when it comes to your head. There can be things going on that don't show physically or that you're un-aware of. Why don't you let me run you over to the ER real quick?"

A strange sound echoed in Oliver's aching ears. Not the howling wind this time, but something else. Something that should not have been there, an odd clicking noise, scratching, like rustling insects, a swarm of shelled bugs furiously scurrying around inside his skull, searching for purchase, or perhaps a way out.

"Oliver?"

His eyes watered in the cold, and he felt a tear roll the length of his cheek.

Your eyes, Oliver…

"Oliver? Are you all right?"

He shook his head, hoping to stop the voices and the scratching sounds scraping the inside of his skull.

Once they find your eyes, just like that tear, that's how they'll escape…

Oliver rubbed his ears with both hands now. "Do you hear that?"

Through your eyes…

A concerned look on his face, Will asked, "You mean the wind?"

The jagged bloody holes where your eyes once were…

The sound faded, absorbed by the howling wind. Oliver stood up and paced about before the bench awkwardly, clouds of breath rolling all around him. "No, I—nothing—my ears are freezing is all."

"We should get out of the cold." Will stood up as well. "I've got to get back soon. Nora has all sorts of projects for me to do this week-end. You know how it is. Let me run you over to the hospital and we'll get this taken care of."

"I don't need to go to the hospital," Oliver said, but deep down he wasn't so sure. Maybe that's exactly what he needed to do. He stood there, feeling useless and weak. "Things are falling apart all around me and I can't stop it."

Responding with a sullen nod, Will said, "I know you don't want to get into it now, but things *have* been tough for you guys lately. Maybe—"

"What are you talking about? Until last night things were fine."

"Okay." Will smiled in what Oliver imagined was meant to be a warm and placating manner, but it came off as sad instead, like Will felt sorry for him. "Then, look, first thing you need to do is find Em-ily. I'm sure she's fine. Who knows, she may even be home by now.

Once you find her, you need to do two more things. One, go to the ER and get checked out thoroughly. And I mean *both* of you, not just Emily. And two, get hold of a lawyer. It sounds like you're going to need one." Will shuffled his feet against the wind and cold, his breath merging with Oliver's to form a single giant tumbling cloud. "I'm sorry, I know you don't want to hear this, Oliver, but you're not exactly acting like yourself either. Here's what I think. Last night was very traumatic and stressful, and maybe both you guys are suffering from some sort of PTSD or something. Plus, you hit your head, and you never know when it comes to things like that. It can lead to all sorts of issues, a lot of which you seem to be suffering from. And before you ask, I'm not saying I don't believe you. I've known you too long. I know you're telling me the truth, at least what you sincerely believe to be the truth. I am concerned, though, and I need you to promise you'll see a doctor ASAP."

"Sure," Oliver said, "I promise."

More lies, he thought. *They're effortless now.*

"Come on," Will said, "let's head back to the cars. I'm frozen."

"You go ahead. I'm going to try calling Emily again."

Will hesitated. "You sure you'll be all right?"

"Yeah, thanks for listening. I'm sorry. I know I sound like a lunatic."

"No you don't. You sound scared. I would be too. These days who isn't?"

"I'll get it worked out."

"And you'll go see a doctor." Will pointed at him like a reprimanding parent. "You promised. If I hear from the cops, I've got your back, no worries. And if you need anything, call me. I'll check in with you later tonight, see what's going on and how you guys are doing, cool?"

"Cool. Thanks."

Will leaned in and gave him a quick, rather awkward hug. Oliver couldn't remember the last time they'd embraced. As he watched Will walk back toward the parking lot, a misty plume of breath trailing him, Oliver turned away, grabbed his cell from his coat pocket and hit Emily's number.

When it began to ring, he noticed the woman on the far side of the pond was no longer looking at the trees. She was looking at him. Motionless as a statue, she watched him, her eyes dead, emotionless, her face expressionless.

"This is Emily, leave a message and I'll get back soon as I can. Thanks!"

Oliver disconnected the call, his arm dropping down to his side as he continued to watch the woman across the pond. His vision blurred in the icy wind, his eyes filled again. But even through the tears, he could see there was something wrong with the woman.

Something impossibly, horribly wrong...

Oliver pawed at his eyes.

Holding the woman's stare, he watched her chest as it rose then fell with a slow and steady rhythm. She was breathing, but unlike his, unlike Will's, unlike anything alive, her breath was not visible in the cold.

10

The SUV was in the driveway. Emily was back.

Oliver pulled in and shut off the engine. Grateful to see nothing out of the ordinary, no unusual cars, no police, none of his neighbors outside, he looked to the sky. Still threatening rain or more snow, it remained an ominous shade of gunmetal gray, and though the fog had dissipated somewhat, it was still fairly heavy. Snaking around the car, it slowly enveloped it, obscuring his view. He rubbed his eyes and took a few deep breaths but his heart continued to race and his hands refused to stop shaking. Visions of the woman in the park still haunted him. Had he really seen what he thought he had? Although impossible, given the events of the last several hours, that hardly seemed to matter.

Stepping from the car, Oliver noticed Gilly was standing in one of his front windows, watching him. Oliver offered a tentative wave. Scowling, Gilly shook his head as if disgusted then moved out of view. Unsure of what that was all about, Oliver hurried through the brutal cold and into the house.

Greeted by a welcome embrace of heat, he saw Emily standing in the kitchen staring at the ceiling. He closed and locked the front door behind him.

"Emily?"

She neither moved nor answered.

Oliver noticed she was dressed in a short skirt, a tight, low-cut sweater and heels. He moved closer, hesitantly, and said her name again.

This time she turned and glanced at him. Thoroughly disinterested in his presence, she returned her attention to the ceiling without further acknowledging him.

Oliver followed her gaze to the ball-shaped light fixture mounted to the ceiling. The bottom half of the fixture was black, and it took a moment of staring at it himself before Oliver realized it was filled with the carcasses of dead bugs. "What the hell?" he muttered. "When did that happen?"

How had so many bugs gotten in there so quickly? Surely if they'd been there the night before he would've seen them. He'd been in the kitchen and turned that same light on several times and hadn't noticed anything in the base of the fixture at all.

"They were drawn to it," Emily said in a dreamy voice. "Drawn to death…"

The woman in the park flashed in Oliver's head.

"To rebirth…"

"What are you talking about?" Oliver looked away from the light, focused on his wife instead. "Emily, where were you? Did you get your prescription filled?"

"I don't need a prescription."

"Ezra said you—"

"Ezra doesn't care about any fool prescription either. Not anymore."

"Not anymore?"

"Leave me alone."

"Where were you this morning?"

"Work," she said absently.

"Today's Saturday," he reminded her. "You don't work on weekends."

She continued staring at the bugs, mesmerized.

"Emily," he said again, touching her arm, "I need to talk to you."

Slowly, her head turned and she met his gaze. "What do you want?"

"Why are you dressed like that? You're not even wearing a bra."

"Don't have any panties on either. You used to like me like this."

Oliver sighed, ran his hands through his hair. "Emily, where did you go?"

"I went to work."

"Your office is closed on weekends."

"I had something I needed to do."

The smell of liquor wafted from her then quickly dissipated. "Have you been drinking?"

"What difference does it make?"

"It's eleven o'clock in the morning."

"So?"

"Why are you dressed like that?" Oliver pressed. "You don't dress like that at work. You can see right through that sweater."

"I want everyone to see my tits. Otherwise I would've worn a bra, genius."

"What the fuck is going on with you?"

Finally looking away from the light fixture, Emily's eyes searched his in a way he'd never before seen. Hers was the cold look of a predator evaluating its prey. "I want to look sexy," she finally answered. "It's important to look sexy. Don't you think I look sexy, Oliver?"

"Why were you drinking if you went in to do some catch-up work at the office? And if you were alone, what difference does it make *what* you look like?"

"Who said I was alone?"

"You were with someone?"

Emily looked back up at the light and smiled.

"Emily, answer me."

"Look at them up there," she said, "trapped in the glass, so many of them you can't tell where one ends and the next begins, it—it's oddly *beautiful*, don't you think?"

"No, I don't. I think it's disgusting and ugly."

"You'll come to find the beauty in it," she said softly.

"What does that mean?"

"Fuck off, that's what it means."

"Did you know the police were here this morning?"

"Don't talk about that right now."

"They know about the hit and—"

"Not now, Oliver."

"A detective sat right in this kitchen and—"

"I *said* don't talk about that right now." Emily spun round as if she'd planned to lunge for him, but only glared at him instead. "We wouldn't want anyone to overhear you just yet, would we?"

"We're the only ones here, Emily."

"No we're not."

Oliver forced a swallow. "Who's here?"

"I made some new friends this morning."

Leaving her to stare at the light fixture, Oliver walked into the den.

Two men sat on the couch, a third in a chair by the window. Oliver had never seen them before. The one in the chair was a thin, casually but nicely dressed man who appeared to be in his fifties, bald but for a horseshoe of gray. The other two were thirtysomethings, rugged and unkempt.

"Hello there," the older man said, smiling with teeth stained a dull gray color. "You must be Emily's husband."

The two on the couch looked over at Oliver and offered quick nods.

"Who are you guys?" Oliver asked, keeping his voice steady as he could.

"Friends," the older man said, still smiling.

"I don't know you."

"Your wife does."

"Look, my wife is—she's not well, she—"

"Seems fine to us," he said, licking his lips. "Just wants a good time is all."

"There's been a misunderstanding." Oliver nervously cleared his throat. "I need you to leave. Right now, you have to leave."

As he rose from the chair, the older man exchanged troubled glances with the others. "I don't think that's what Emily wants."

"I don't care what Emily wants. Get out of my house."

The two guys on the couch stood up, looking more inconvenienced and annoyed than angry. They looked to the older man, as if for instruction.

"Why don't you go ask Emily if we should leave?" the man said.

Oliver hadn't been in a physical confrontation since junior high school, but fear and anger were powerful things. Where the hell had he left that baseball bat? "Look, I don't know how you know my wife, but—"

"I told you, we're friends," he said, that inane smile still in place. "We met this morning at a place downtown, had some drinks and a little fun. Actually, a whole lot of fun. You're a lucky man, friend."

"I'm not your friend."

"She invited us here. Said you might be around but it wasn't a big deal."

"She's wrong, it is a big deal. Get out."

"Wow, seems like we got off on the wrong foot here," the man said. "Hate to say it, but this is a whole lot easier with your wife. She's much friendlier than you are. As a matter of fact, she's *so* friendly we know exactly what she wants. The sexy little slut's been asking for it since we met her. She even brought us back here so she'd be sure to get it."

"Watch your mouth, asshole."

"We already watched Emily's earlier." He grinned lasciviously. "Like I said, you're a lucky man."

"I'm warning you."

"We're not going anywhere. *I'm* warning *you*."

Oliver stormed back into the kitchen, where he found Emily leaned against the counter, a drink in her hand. She'd kicked her heels off and was apparently no longer concerned with the light fixture. "Are you out of your *fucking* mind? You picked up three strange men and brought them to our *home*?"

Emily's eyes widened as if amused. "Don't you like my new friends?"

"I'm calling the police."

"I wouldn't do that if I were you."

It felt as if she'd punched him in the gut. "Are you *threatening* me?"

"Oh, Oliver, don't be such a wuss." She rolled her eyes. "Have a drink."

"You had sex with these fucking guys?"

"Depends on how you want to define sex," she laughed, as if it meant nothing at all, as if his pain was not only unimportant, but amusing.

"I don't—I can't believe this, I—"

"Chill out and have some fun with us. God knows you've got nowhere to go or anything else to do."

"What the hell is that supposed to mean?"

"What do you think it means, you little bitch?"

"Get those guys out of here. *Now*, I mean it."

"Stop trying to be a tough guy, Oliver." Emily sipped her drink. "You don't scare anyone and you sound ridiculous. Besides, it's just blowjobs. Nobody's in love. Fucking relax."

In all the years Oliver had known her, he'd never seen Emily laugh at him like that. "Who are you? What in God's name is happening to us?"

"I'm having a party, that's what's happening." Emily padded closer to him in her bare feet. "Don't you want to come to my party, Oliver?"

"You're not having any party, and no, I don't."

"Oops, it already started. I guess I forgot to invite you." She leaned in, brushed her lips across his neck on her way to his ear, and whispered, "So get out. Or I'll have them throw you out."

"Emily, look at me," he said, blocking her way out of the kitchen.

As she did, Oliver looked deep into her eyes, searching for the woman he knew was still in there somewhere. "I love you."

"I know you do," she said softly.

He reached out carefully and took her free hand. "And you love me."

Emily nodded, as if mistakenly, and then staggered back and slumped against the counter. "I'm so tired all of a sudden, I…I'm so *tired*, Oliver."

He helped her over to the table and down into one of the chairs, then grabbed his phone. Oliver decided to call Stan. He'd help, and even though he was older, he was the kind of guy who could get these men out of his house. But then it occurred to him that he had no idea what Stan's number was. Neighbors all this time and he didn't even know his phone number.

Ezra's words from the other night rang in his ears.

We're not friends, Oliver. I barely know you.

"Is everything okay in here?"

The older man stood in the doorway, smiling; the other two behind him.

Oliver brought his phone to his ear. "I'm calling the police," he said. "You guys better get out of here."

"We were invited. Weren't we, Emily? Tell him, doll."

Emily remained slumped over at the table, her head in her hands as if she were suffering from a terrible headache. "Leave," she said in a loud whisper. "Get the fuck out of our house."

"Crazy whore," the man chuckled.

"It's ringing," Oliver said.

"Come on now," the man said to Oliver. "We rode here with her. How are we supposed to get back to our cars at the bar? It's on the other side of town."

"I hear Uber's nice." Oliver pointed to the door. "Get out."

"All right, all right, be cool, we're going." The man laughed lightly, looking past Oliver to Emily. "Maybe next time, huh, doll? Thanks for the laughs."

"Yes, hello," Oliver said, pretending he'd been connected to the police.

The three men filed out the door quickly.

Oliver closed it behind them, locked it and fell back against it. He stood there a moment, waiting for his heartrate to return to normal, then went back to Emily and crouched down next to her.

"Come on," he said, "I'm taking you to the hospital."

"You should've killed them. Why didn't you kill them?"

"What? I—I just wanted them out of our house."

"Even after what happened?"

"What do you want from me, Emily?"

"Everything...Nothing...Your blood...and mine...all over me."

"We're getting you to a doctor, right now."

"I just want to go to bed, Oliver."

"No, come on, I'll help you to the car."

"I have to sleep. Please." She took his hands in hers. "*Please*, Oliver."

Angry, hurt and frightened, he held his wife's hands. He'd never felt more lost. "Emily..."

"I have to sleep. Even then I have such horrible dreams...such... *terrible* dreams...but all he can do is torment me if I'm asleep, he—he can't make me do things like when I'm awake. I'd rather have the nightmares, I'd rather—"

"Come on, we're going to the ER. Right now, we're going now. Let's get your shoes on."

Emily grabbed hold of his wrist with both hands. Her grip was so strong it hurt. "I can feel it," she whispered, as if fearful someone might hear. "I can feel *him*. Inside me, Oliver, I can feel him, moving through my blood. I'm trying to fight him but he's getting stronger. He's *inside* me."

His heart breaking, Oliver didn't know whether to destroy everything in the room in an uncontrollable rage or to break down in tears. Emily looked and sounded completely insane. And there was nothing he could do about it.

"He's *inside* me," she said again. "It's not me, it's—it's him. He's the one doing this, making—making *me* do this. I'm sorry, baby, I—I'm so sorry, I—I don't want any of this. *He* does."

Oliver already knew the answer but asked anyway. "The man in the fedora?"

"He's not a man." Tears spilled across Emily's cheeks, smearing her dark eye makeup into long black streaks that stained her face like war paint. "He's not human, Oliver. He's not *human*."

No, he's not, Oliver thought. *But are you?*

PART TWO

"It was a strange time. You had a president who'd corrupted an election talking about threats to democracy...Despite the anti-war meetings and demos we attended, Judith and I both felt a sense of frozen helplessness. It was as if ordinary people no longer existed."

—Joel Lane, *The Witnesses Are Gone*

11

By the time Oliver had gotten Emily into bed and she'd drifted off to sleep, or something similar, someone had begun knocking on the front door. Assuming Emily would be all right for the time being, Oliver hurried downstairs to answer what had quickly escalated into an aggressive pounding.

He opened the door to see Gilly standing there, frowning and with his arms folded across his chest. "Everything all right over here?" he asked in a tone closer to irritable than concerned.

"Yeah, I—just—Emily's not feeling well."

Gilly weighed the validity of Oliver's response longer than seemed warranted. "Sorry to hear that. Melinda's been under the weather too."

"Well, I hope she feels better, but I have to go, I—"

"That's not the reason I'm here. Been an awful lot of activity over here since this morning, want to make sure there isn't something going on I need to be aware of. And before you say it's none of my business, if something's taking place in the neighborhood where my wife and I live, then it *is* my business."

"I don't have time for this right now, Stan."

"I saw Emily pull in with those guys and—"

"They're gone."

"I know, saw them leave on foot. Not the most savory looking crowd I've ever laid eyes on." Gilly smirked. "Not sure what *that* was all about, and I'm sure I don't want to know, but—"

"It's nothing to be concerned about, okay?"

"Hey, if you don't care why the hell should I? I was more concerned about the other guy anyway."

Oliver stepped out into the cold and quietly closed the door behind him. "What other guy?"

"Not sure who he was, thought maybe he was someone you know. Never got a good look at his face, but he looked older, wore a long winter coat and a hat, both black."

"What kind of hat?"

"Fedora, like the gangsters wore in the old movies, you know the kind. Back when movies were good and had real stars like Edward G. and Jimmy Cagney, not these namby-pamby wannabe—"

"When was this?"

"Showed up a few minutes after you left this morning," Gilly explained. "I don't know what it was, just something about the guy that didn't set right with me. Not saying he did anything wrong necessarily, least not that I saw, but he made me uneasy. Just stood here at your door, for one thing, then after a minute, he knocked a few times. Even when it was obvious no one was going to answer the door, he kept hanging around, just standing there, know what I mean? Right where I am now, staring at your door like a loon."

"Did you talk to him?"

"Never got the chance," Gilly said. "Went to get my jacket, but by the time I got outside he was gone. I checked your property thoroughly, trust me, walked and inspected the entire perimeter. Under the circumstances, didn't think you'd mind. Thought maybe the guy went around back, couldn't find a trace of him, though. Anyway, I've never seen him before, and add to that his bizarre behavior, and you can understand my concern. Is this guy a friend of yours?"

Oliver couldn't seem to get himself to stop shaking. The man in the fedora was real, he knew that now. Someone else had seen him. And not only was he real, he'd found them. Every instinct he had told him to run, to get Emily and get as far from here as they could. But where would they go? Where *could* they go? "No, I—I don't think so, he—he doesn't sound familiar."

"What's wrong?" Gilly moved closer, so close they were only a few inches apart. "You look like you're about to come out of your skin. What's the matter with you?"

Oliver shook his head, unsure of how to respond.

"Did something happen with those guys Emily came home with?"

"That was just a misunderstanding."

A smile slowly creased Gilly's lips. "I bet."

"I took care of it, they—they're gone."

"The other guy," Gilly said, smile fading, "he means something to you."

"I have to go inside now."

"What'd that fat cop want with you?"

"Nothing, just—I need to go, Stan."

"Tell me what's going on."

"I don't know. I don't know what you mean."

"Sure you do," Gilly said through suddenly gritted teeth. "You just don't want to tell me. Maybe you *can't* tell me, least not yet. But you will eventually. Know why? Because even though you think I'm a Cro-Magnon buffoon too stupid to be as highly intellectual and forward-thinking as you, I'm exactly what you need when things go wrong and you start to realize your highfalutin *bullshit* isn't worth the planet-friendly, recycled, hypoallergenic dye- and bleach-free paper it's printed on. Guys like you run to guys like me, even though until you need us, you make fun of us and treat us like morons unworthy of your oh-so-serious and important attention."

"No more than you need men like me when your simplistic crap runs its course and loses its effectiveness. You know, when you actually need someone who's maybe read something beyond comics and popup books and has some semblance of education and intellect."

"Okay, snowflake, take it easy."

"You take it easy, you fascist clown."

"Fucking pussy."

"Goon."

"Faggot!"

"Bigot!"

"Commie!"

"Nazi!"

Somehow, it seemed to Oliver, wherever that thing in the fedora was, it was smiling, pleased with this mayhem. Perhaps it even fed on it.

85

The men stood there a while, glaring at each other like two children in conflict on a playground. Oliver had no doubt Gilly wanted to punch him just then, but what surprised him was how much he wanted to do the same to Gilly. In all the time they'd known each other there had always been some tension and awkwardness to their interactions, but nothing that indicated such vitriol existed in either of them, and so close to the surface.

"This is ridiculous," Oliver finally said. "I didn't mean to—"

"Yeah, okay." Very slowly, Gilly stood down. "Me either."

For a brief moment, Oliver considered trusting him with everything. "Look, Stan, I—"

"Sometimes I think the only thing guys like you and guys like me have in common is pretending we don't ever need each other," Gilly said, the previous intensity and aggression in his tone all but gone. "Truth is we both got our place, and we probably all have a lot more in common than we think."

"Or like to admit," Oliver added.

Gilly glanced back at the street, as if expecting to see someone else approaching. "You really think I'm a fascist clown?"

"Do you really think I'm a snowflake pussy?"

"Kind of, yeah," Gilly said, laughing clumsily. "That doesn't necessarily make you a bad guy, though. Sorry, that's the best I got at the moment."

"I'll take it." Oliver offered his hand.

Gilly shook his hand. "All I'm saying is, I got to live here too, Oliver. I got a right to know if something's going on that can affect me or my wife."

"I understand."

"Give me your word if there's something I need to know you'll tell me."

"I give you my word, Stan."

After a moment, apparently satisfied, he let Oliver's hand go. "How come you never call me Gilly?"

"I don't know. I've just always called you Stan."

"Well my friends call me *Gilly*, so, you know…"

"Sure," Oliver said. "Okay. Thanks."

"No hard feelings, that's what I'm saying over here."

"All right, me too."

"Okay then." Gilly sighed. "I got to get home, like I said, Melinda's not feeling well either. Not sure what her problem is. Last couple days all she wants to do is sleep, day and night. Never seen anybody that's not a baby sleep like that, you know? Cranky as all getup too, mean as a snake lately, and that's not like her. Mostly wants to be left alone, so I've been staying out of her way." He gave Oliver a playful nudge with his elbow. "Must be that time of month, huh? Never trust anything that bleeds for a week and don't die, am I right?"

As Gilly started back down the walkway, Oliver grabbed his arm. "Wait."

"You want to let go of me, chief?" Gilly glanced down at Oliver's hand clamped onto his arm. "Thought we had things all worked out, but that's quite a grip you got there. Not exactly comfortable, get my drift?"

"I'm sorry." Oliver snatched his hand back. "Did Melinda see him too, the man in the fedora?"

"I don't see how she could've. She was in bed when I saw him." Gilly's eyes narrowed. "Why?"

"Nothing, I just thought maybe she'd seen him too."

"I understand English, it's my first language. My question was *why?*"

Reaching behind him, Oliver opened the door. "It's just that Emily's been behaving the same way," he said. "Lots of sleep and all, she—she's sleeping now actually."

"What's that got to do with our friend in the hat?"

"Nothing," Oliver answered, feigning nonchalance.

"Then why'd—"

"Why would it have anything to do with some guy at my door?"

Gilly stared at him. "Wait. *You* asked if—"

"Tell Melinda I hope she feels better. Must be something going around."

"Yeah," Gilly said, eyeing him suspiciously, "must be, huh?"

"I have to go."

"Just remember our deal, Oliver. You gave me your word. End of the day, it's all we got. If a man doesn't have that, then he's nothing. What the hell good is he, am I right?"

Oliver watched as Gilly strode back down the walk and toward his house. Looking ahead of him, he thought he saw someone in one of the front windows of Gilly's house, but due to the drawn curtains it was only a quickly moving shadow, there then gone, if it had ever truly been there at all.

Melinda was watching us, Oliver thought.

Closing the door, Oliver staggered through the kitchen and over to the counter. Falling against it, his head pounding, he tried to calm his frayed nerves and decide what to do next.

And then the phone began to ring.

After a deep breath, Oliver answered. "Hello?"

"Mr. Young?"

He recognized the voice immediately. "Yes?"

"Detective Joan Brenda, we spoke earlier?"

"Yes, I—what can I do for you?"

"I hadn't heard from Mrs. Young and was hoping maybe she'd returned home by now and I might be able to have a quick chat with her."

"I'm afraid she isn't feeling very well."

"She is at home, then?"

"Yes, but she's resting now. She's sleeping, actually."

He could hear her breathing through the phone, but nothing more.

"Detective?" he asked the silence, his grip on the phone tightening. It felt as if she were watching him somehow, through the phone line. "Hello?"

"When she's up and about, have her give me a ring, please."

Before he could respond the line clicked and disconnected.

Oliver hung the phone up and rubbed his eyes. His head was still pounding and he needed to take something. But before he could make his way to the bathroom, the phone rang again.

He answered quickly. "Yes?"

Heavy breathing, nothing more...

"Hello?"

A noise that began as something similar to a whisper swept through the phone, slowly morphing into a jumble of electronic sounds. Oliver pulled the phone from his ear as they became an unbearable screech. Holding the phone out in front of him, he listened as the alien sounds continued, finally softening and changing again, this time into a voice caught somewhere between synthetic and male human.

Cautiously, he brought the phone back to his ear, hearing only a quiet hiss now. "Hello?"

"You and your wife are not alone in the house."

A chill pranced along the base of his skull. "Who is this?"

The call disconnected, leaving only dead air, so Oliver pressed *69 and waited to see where the call had originated from. Whoever it was, he'd call the bastard back and find out who he was and why he was doing this.

"The number you are trying to reach is not in service," a canned voice told him. "Please check the number and call again."

Oliver slammed the phone back on the wall and clenched shut his eyes.

Horrible visions of Emily with those men flooded his head, worsening his headache. He needed a couple aspirin before it got out of control and became debilitating. As he went to the sink and turned on the faucet to get a glass of water, he looked out through the windows into the backyard.

At the very edge of their property, just inside the tree line, a woman he recognized immediately as the one he'd seen in the park stood motionless in the fog, watching the house.

Oliver turned the faucet off and quickly made his way to the back door. Unlocking then swinging it open, he looked again, this time through the storm door. The woman was still there.

Stepping outside and into the cold, Oliver slowly descended the two small steps to the patio. The woman had seen him now too, but didn't move or acknowledge him in any way. Her breath was still not forming clouds in the air, and he was certain she had not blinked in the entire time they'd been looking at each other.

Despite his terror, Oliver moved across the small yard until he was only about twenty feet from the woman.

"Who are you?" he asked. "Did you follow me here?"

The woman was still staring at him, only now she looked baffled, and perhaps even a bit frightened.

Like the man she was looking at was completely insane.

"*What do you want?*" Oliver's body shuddered from what he kept telling himself was the cold. "What do you want?"

The woman's mouth fell open, almost as if it had done so against her will, but still, there was no visible breath escaping her.

"You're not alone in the house," a male voice from within her said.

The same voice he'd just heard on the phone.

Her mouth snapped shut, teeth clacking as her body began to violently shake and convulse. Things small, dark and insect-like emerged from her, crawling out from the bottoms of her eyes, pouring free by the dozens and streaming across her face to the frozen ground below.

That's how they'll escape, Oliver...through your eyes...

Nearly losing his balance, Oliver staggered back in a frenzied attempt to back away from her as quickly as possible. Catching himself at the last moment, he avoided falling then looked to the abomination again.

The jagged bloody holes where your eyes once were...

As the things that emerged from her eyes scurried off in various directions, the woman turned and began running back through the forest, her gait awkward and forced, as if her body had never performed such a function and was unfamiliar with how to do so.

Certain all sanity had deserted him, Oliver spun away in a frantic pirouette, stumbled madly then again found his balance. Breaking into a run, he dashed for the house.

12

Running…Oliver remembered running. Just steps from the house, a horrible pain fired through his head. Like a spike stabbed through his forehead, it exploded into his temples, dropping him to his knees. He tried for the door, but it remained just out of reach as the horrible sounds behind him—the clicking of thousands of shelled insects—scurried closer.

Darkness fell over him like a cloak, blinding him and leaving only the terrible sensation of falling hopelessly into night. A darkness unlike anything he'd known before, this darkness was endless, with no beginning, no end and no way out. Worse, this darkness was *alive*. He could feel it slithering all around him like a nest of snakes, wrapping around him and tightening into a cold and horrible embrace.

Oliver screamed.

He tasted the night, the rot, the death and hopelessness of the damned. Like dirt from ancient graves, the evil poured down over him. And it was then that he realized the darkness had tricked him. It had been trying to get inside him all along. Now it had.

And he'd let it in.

* * *

Oliver awakened to the echo of slow, methodical footfalls.

The pain in his head remained, but had become more centralized to his temples. His neck and shoulders were stiff and sore, and he felt vaguely sick to his stomach. It took several seconds for him to realize he was in a steel chair of some kind that appeared to be bolted to the floor. He'd been strapped into it, and it wasn't until Oliver tried to move that he felt the pain. He attempted to look down but couldn't even turn his head. Some sort of metal device had been attached to his skull and held in place with what he guessed by feel were screws or something similar turned tight to his temples. With the torturous device fastened to his head, Oliver could only look straight ahead. Sitting in a room, the only light a dim wash from the adjacent hallway just outside the open door, he could barely make out the hallway in his peripheral vision. But someone was walking out there, coming closer and shining what he thought might be a flashlight, the beam swinging back and forth as if looking for something.

As he again attempted to wiggle free, the pain became excruciating. Lowering his eyes and trembling uncontrollably, he realized his hands and feet were bound with barbed wire. Fear rose in him again, joining the pain as his wrists and ankles began to bleed. He knew if he lost control the barbed wire would rip him to shreds, so despite his terror, Oliver did his best to stay still.

He thought he might lose consciousness, perhaps even hoped he might, but though his vision had blurred slightly, he remained awake as his eyes slowly focused in the relative darkness.

Looking about as best he could, Oliver saw the floor was an industrial tile, the walls and ceilings a dull tan color, the paint chipped and badly peeling. One small section of floor in front of his chair consisted of a metal grate instead of tile and was outfitted with a narrow trough running along its side. It reminded him of something one might find in a slaughterhouse, yet the room had the feel and look of a hospital of some kind, one old and long ago abandoned.

Before Oliver could think more about it, a large electronic screen came to life a few feet directly in front of him, at eye-level, spilling light and deafening sounds into the small room.

A rapid montage of sights and sounds played across the screen.

A police officer screaming at a young black man on his knees, his hands in the air…the cop screaming for him to stop resisting…the booming sound of gunfire, and a guttural noise somewhere between a cry and a deep grunt from the man shot…the officer emptying his gun even after the man had fallen back and lay still in a growing pool of blood…

"What is this?" Oliver screeched and slammed shut his eyes, only to open them again a second later. This time he saw a vision of himself on the screen, as more horrible scenes played out before and all around him.

Oliver watched himself running down a hallway, perhaps the same one just outside the room he found himself in; unsure of where he was going or where it led, he ran as fast as he could, confused and horrified and unable to make sense of what was happening.

Suddenly something caught his leg. He saw himself trip and vault forward, landing hard on his stomach and sliding several feet through the darkness along the hallway floor. Scrambling to his feet, he looked back long enough to see that he'd fallen over the severed limb of what appeared to be a human being.

Even when he'd begun to struggle to free himself from the chair, pain ripping at his flesh, he continued to watch himself onscreen, unable to look away.

The screen version charged forward, running down the hallway, but the farther he ran the more dilapidated and ravaged the building around him became, and the more carnage he encountered. Soon the entire floor was covered in pieces of human beings that had been blown apart and dismembered with unimaginable violence. Men, women—even children—of every description lay dead at his feet, in pieces. As he vomited and slipped, sliding through the blood and entrails, Oliver regained his footing and kept running. All around him the sounds of newscasts, or something similar, echoed through the hallway, ghostlike and gruesome, voice layered upon voice describing wars and bombings, terrorist attacks and various atrocities across the globe, as well as protestors in the streets, cities aflame and the gleeful malevolent frenzy of nationalist rallies, the endless droning of so-called pundits and spokespeople, liars and racists, humorless social justice warriors and angry rednecks waving traitorous flags, limousine liberals, rightwing extremists, wannabe anarchists and entitled, falsely righteous narcissists living in protective bubbles, the vehement angry diatribes of supporters from all political bents and the loss of any rational, critical or reasonable thought. Context and intent a thing of the past, leaving only rage, violence and hatred—*fear*—a world offended by everything but ashamed of nothing, torn to shreds not by some outside threat but from within and by its own. No reason or moderation, no understanding or empathy, no second chances, mindless allies or ruthless archenemies all, no middle ground, no shades of gray, just never-ending cycles of finger-pointing, fearmongering, hatred, anger and violence. And all of it led by an assortment of abominations, hideous evils proudly helming a ship of fools toward their own demise.

It all grew louder and louder, like the endlessly escalating and mindless argument it was, raining down on him like bombs, deafening and sending Oliver spinning deeper and deeper into darkness.

Until finally, *gratefully*, the screen went dark…and then…

Silence…

It was perhaps the kindest thing Oliver had ever heard.

But it too was a lie, because he was not alone in the silence any more than he was alone outside the light. He could feel the man in the fedora there too. Separating from the darkness, he grabbed hold of Oliver and pulled him close, like a lover, his breath hot and rancid against the side of his face.

"Please," Oliver gasped, shuddering. As claws gently traced the carotid artery along the side of his neck, caressing it with a nearly loving touch, his eyes rolled back to white. "What are you?"

Drooling spittle thick and acidic, it whispered in his ear. "*Doom…*"

* * *

Whispers…things moving…clicking…swimming in his blood… through the tattered remnants of his tortured mind…

I'm cold. So cold, so—I'm so cold—

Oliver found himself on the floor in the kitchen, near the back door. On his stomach, he tried to crawl but couldn't muster the strength. Ahead of him, the front door was open, revealing the night, the empty walkway and dark street beyond. Why was the door open? It was freezing in the house, and he knew then why he was shivering so. And yet, his entire body was covered in a slick film of perspiration, as if he were in the throes of a fever.

Strange music played somewhere nearby, ancient and deadly, like a ghostly wind, seductive and slow, dreamlike, it crept through the house, drifting, a drug shot directly into his veins, the syringe backing up with a swirl of blood as he took the fear, pain, and sex into his system. Primitive longings all, he rode them, followed them, a lemming edging slowly toward a cliff, and as he spiraled down, embracing the evil, swallowing it, beyond the open door, in a darkness lit only by the moon, Oliver saw him.

Standing in the street, watching the house, watching *him*, the man in the fedora, eyes glowing red as the blood surging through Oliver's veins, pulsing in his neck, seeking escape…deliverance…

The music swelled, and to his right, Emily appeared, floating slowly down the stairs like an apparition. Dressed in red from head to toe, arms extended out on either side of her, one foot atop another, her head swaying back and forth to the rhythm of the music, a crucified angel taking flight, she glided closer.

Her feet were not touching the ground.

Oliver looked to the door.

The man in the fedora was on the curb now, still watching in the moonlight.

Emily's bare feet touched down at the base of the stairs, and as she danced, the music inside her now, moving her body for her, she twirled without restraint, a seductress overtaken by lust and dripping with the same evil Oliver felt strangling him with pleasure, pain, and horror.

As her body, a body he knew every inch of, swayed and moved to the music, he realized Emily was not dressed in red after all. She was covered in blood. Slick, wet and thick, it covered her otherwise nude body, her eyes two white orbs in a world of crimson, wild and alive but not like any living thing he'd seen before. He feared her, and yet was uncontrollably attracted to her as well, wanting her, needing her…

The man in the fedora was on the walkway, moving closer.

Whispers from countless souls filled Oliver's head, the lost and the damned, calling him, beckoning…

Following the beat, Emily slowly moved her head back and forth. Her hair, wet and matted with blood, sprayed the air around her in a fine mist. Running her hands the length of her torso, up and down then back again, to the sides of her breasts, as the music took her deeper, her eyes closed.

Head thrown back, her body moved like a snake.

No longer cold, Oliver struggled onto all-fours, the fever burning deep within him. Raising his head, he looked again to the door.

The man in the fedora was in the house now, standing in the kitchen, the brim of his hat pulled down to effectively conceal his face.

Hands touched him, wet and warm and sticky. Hands he knew well.

Emily's breath beat down in quick surges against the back of his neck as her arms wrapped around him from behind. Rather than pull him to his feet, she straddled his body with her own, and he braced himself to accommodate her weight. She slid across him, crushing her body against his, still writhing dreamily to the music.

"Do you know his secret?" she whispered, the words slurred by the blood pouring from her mouth. "Do you know his secret name?"

Oliver closed his eyes, but only fire greeted him there. Great pluming swells of it launching from darkness, surrounding an ancient temple lost in an ocean of fire. And at its summit, Emily's eyes emerged against the backdrop of blood and flames. White, wide and crazed, alive with feral, demonic glee.

"Do you feel its *hunger?*"

God help me…yes…

Emily's lips brushed his throat, leaving behind a trail of blood, like a slug. "Do you feel it inside you?"

No…

"Let it love you, Oliver. Give yourself to it, and see how beautiful it is."

Stop…

As his vision cleared, Oliver saw something moving in the darkness on the other side of the room. White and graceful, as if dancing, it fluttered then fell, only to rise again. He found himself aching and shivering, his breath visible in the cold, and realized he was alone in bed beneath a pile of heavy blankets.

The window on the far wall of their bedroom was partially open, the curtain fluttering in the night breeze like a ghost.

Oliver heard sudden movement in the hallway.

He focused on the sliver of light leaking from beneath the bedroom door.

Something moved into its path, blocking it.

And then, very slowly, the door opened.

13

"Are you having bad dreams, Oliver?"

Though unable to see beyond the harsh and sudden light spilling into the room from behind her, the voice and the silhouette in the doorway could only belong to Emily. The sweat poured from him, and he wearily wiped his face and neck as he struggled up into a semi-sitting position.

"Why am I in bed?" Oliver asked. "How did I—"

"Are you having bad dreams, Oliver?" she asked, still just a dark silhouette in the doorway.

"I…I can't tell if I'm dreaming or awake anymore."

"Are you having bad dreams, Oliver?"

"Why do you keep saying that? I'm sick. I feel sick."

"You have to wait."

"Wait?"

"For the bad dreams to end," she told him, face expressionless, tone empty and void of emotion. "Once they end, it begins."

"What begins?"

"And then you realize the bad dreams aren't dreams at all." Emily stepped from the doorway, closer to the bed, but he still couldn't make out anything but shadows. "You realize bad is good, because nothing matters anymore, Oliver, nothing has in quite some time."

"I don't understand."

"You don't remember. But you will."

"Remember what, I—"

"There is only this now."

Oliver's head was pounding, and the perspiration wetting down his body had grown worse. He ran a hand through his hair. It too was soaked with sweat.

"You'll understand when the time is right," Emily said. "We all do."

"*We?*"

She whispered something in response, but he couldn't make it out.

"Come closer," he said breathlessly, "I can't see you."

As Emily leaned into the light from the hallway, her face was partially revealed. She smiled at him. Her mouth and teeth were coated with blood.

"You have blood all over your mouth."

She smiled, accentuating it, and then ran her tongue through the blood, slurping it deeper into her mouth. "It's all right to be afraid. Fear is good. You'll come to know it, to embrace and use it not only to strengthen yourself, but as a weapon against others. The weak and the misguided, the forgotten and the lonely, they eat fear like suckling infants. You're feeding on it right now, so much of it you're choking on it, gagging on it."

Dizzy and reeling from what he could only imagine was a high fever, Oliver grimaced. "Are you going to kill me?"

Emily's eyes narrowed thoughtfully, and for just a second, Oliver recognized the woman he knew and loved. She was in there somewhere, but in bits and pieces, mistaken reminders of who she'd once been. "Why would I kill you?" she asked, as if the question had hurt her. "I love you."

He'd already begun to mourn her. He knew that now.

"Get dressed and come downstairs, my love," she said.

"Why?"

"Come and see." Emily stepped back into the doorway. "Come and see."

Vanishing into the glare of light, she closed the door behind her, returning the bedroom to darkness.

Oliver kicked away the blankets and swung his feet around to the floor. Only then did he realize he was nude. Switching on the nightstand lamp, light punched a hole in the darkness sufficient enough for him to make out a pile of clothes on the floor nearby. At some point he'd undressed—or been undressed—before getting in or being put to bed, and his clothes had remained where they'd fallen.

In the limited light, he inspected his body as best he could. Another wave of dizziness swept through him, and he was still quite weak. Satisfied he hadn't sustained any wounds, Oliver forced himself from bed. Gathering his clothes, he quickly dressed then grabbed his wallet from the nightstand.

Leaning against the bed, he waited until the dizziness left him.

Oliver opened the bedroom door. The hall light had been extinguished, but there was enough light from downstairs to partially illuminate the hallway. He hesitated just outside the doorway and heard the soft murmur of voices coming from downstairs as well. Although still mostly shadows, Oliver knew the hallway well enough to negotiate it by rote, so he crept forward, his hand against the interior wall for support until he reached the head of the staircase.

Crouching, he steadied himself against the bannister as another wave of dizziness hit. Dripping perspiration, Oliver carefully lay flat on his stomach and peered down into the living room.

Emily stood near the windows, looking out into the night as if waiting for someone else to arrive. The men he'd thrown out earlier were there, as were Ezra and Maureen Adelson. Will and Nora were there too. In fact, nearly everyone who'd attended their party the other night was there as well, including Arthur, of all people. The group was talking amongst themselves in hushed tones, so Oliver couldn't make out anything specific but for a word here or there. Whatever they were discussing was deadly serious, as no one was laughing or even smiling. Instead, everyone appeared somber, the way those attending a wake or funeral might.

Why was Will there? He said he'd call Oliver to check in but never had. And what the hell was Arthur doing in their house? Emily never would've invited him. She couldn't stand Arthur.

Remaining where he was, Oliver watched as Emily came away from the window and struck up a hushed conversation with Will and Nora.

Whatever was happening here, everyone in his living room was in on it. There could be no denying that now. They were all a part of it.

Quietly, Oliver crawled back toward the bedroom, then managed to get to his feet. Though still a little lightheaded, the dizziness was nearly gone. He was soaked with perspiration but no longer sweating as profusely as he had been earlier, so he slipped back into the bedroom and grabbed a jacket from the closet. In one of his bureau drawers he found an old knit hat he rarely wore and pulled it on. Sitting at the foot of the bed, he tried to figure out how to best get out of the house.

There was only one way to the first floor, and that was down the stairs and straight into the heart of Emily's little gathering, so that was out.

The only other option was escaping through a second-floor window.

Even if he made it, Oliver had no idea where he'd go. Perhaps if he could make it outside into the cold fresh air and put some distance between himself and whatever was going on, his head would clear and he could think straight.

Regardless, all he knew for sure was that one way or another, he had to get out of that house, and fast. It was only a matter of time before Emily or one of the others came looking for him again.

Oliver went to the window, looked down into the side yard.

It wasn't an enormous drop, but too far to jump safely, and he couldn't risk hurting himself in the fall.

Think, goddamn it. There has to be a way.

If he couldn't go down…maybe he could go up.

Oliver unlocked the window and slid it open. The screen was still on. Each winter he changed them over to storm windows, but he hadn't yet gotten around to it. Quietly, he lifted the screen then yanked it free of its tracks. Tilting it sideways, he pulled the screen into the bedroom.

Tossing it on the bed, he returned to the window and stuck his head out into the cold night. He immediately felt the chill hit his face and nostrils, and it jolted him more awake and focused. He breathed in the fresh air then looked up at the slope of the roof overhead. The gutter was within reach. If he could get a solid grip and pull himself up and onto the roof, he could then follow it to the back of the house. There, above the kitchen, the roof was no longer slanted and was also significantly closer to the ground than the pitched section. If he could make it that far, he could likely drop down onto the patio without hurting himself.

Oliver wished he had more of his strength back, but he had no choice.

He was running out of time.

Sitting on the windowsill, he leaned out into the moonlight. He climbed up and into position, then reached for the gutter, hopeful it would hold his weight long enough for him to pull himself free of the window and up onto the roof.

He clamped his hands onto the cold gutter, giving it a little pull to test its strength. The entire section bowed and gave more than he was comfortable with. Rather than think about it, Oliver pushed with his legs and pulled hard as he could. Launching himself out and up in a single awkward motion, his legs suddenly dangled in space. He leaned hard into the edge of the roof, hands now pinned beneath his chest and still clutching the gutter.

A cracking sound cut the night as the gutter shifted.

Oliver quickly swung a leg up onto the roof. The gutter shifted again as his foot caught the edge. Using it for leverage, he forced himself up and into place. The gutter buckled, holding just long enough for him to crawl free of it and higher onto the slanted roof.

Rolling onto his back and out of breath, Oliver looked down past his feet to see that the section of gutter he'd used had separated from the house. It hadn't fallen or come completely free, but another few seconds and he and it would've plummeted to the ground.

Carefully, Oliver got himself onto all fours and climbed the slant to the summit of the roof. He rose to his feet and looked around. He hadn't been on a roof since he was a kid and realized in that moment that he'd never been on this one in all the years they'd lived here. There was something peculiar and alien about it, a perspective one wasn't meant to have in any natural or usual sense. He didn't belong up here. No one did.

Nothing human, at least…

This was his house, his neighborhood, his town, and yet, he felt like a stranger, a visitor that had no business or connection here. But here he was.

The neighborhood was quiet and dark. He could see for miles, and there was something at once oddly freeing and deeply troubling about that.

Distant lights twinkled, and Oliver wondered about the people in all those houses. What were they doing? What was happening in their lives? Were there others like him out there who had no idea what was going on?

What the hell am I doing?

Late at night, up on his roof like a madman, attempting to escape his own home. How had his world come to this? How had it all gone so bad, so quickly?

Just a day ago he'd been happy—*they'd* been happy—hadn't they?

I know you don't want to get into it now, but things have been tough for you guys lately...

And now everything had gone insane.

God knows you've got nowhere to go or anything else to do...

Or perhaps he had.

I can't tell if I'm dreaming or awake or anymore...

Oliver tried to focus on the night. He listened. If anyone had heard him they would've been in the bedroom by now, poking their head out of the open window looking for him. There would've been some commotion by now.

Instead, except for the storms in his head, the night was deathly quiet.

And then, suddenly, from below, someone screamed.

The doors at the front and back of the house burst open in unison, spilling first light and then people into the night.

Oliver crouched low, so as not to be seen if anyone looked up, horrified as everyone in the house ran out into the darkness, streaming free of it furiously, like rats fleeing fire.

Screeching like banshees, some ran into the woods across the street, others into the woods out back, and more still down to the end of the cul-de-sac and into the road.

They'd found the bedroom empty. They knew he was gone. But from their reactions, they'd assumed he'd dropped down to the ground and run, as not one of them looked to the roof.

Careful to keep his footfalls soft as possible, just in case anyone had stayed behind in the house, Oliver crept across the roof, down the other side and onto the flat portion over the kitchen. When he was close enough, he dropped down onto the seat of his pants and crab-walked to the edge.

The forest behind the house was dark, and those who had run into the woods to find him were nowhere in sight. With his heart beating so hard he was having trouble drawing a full breath, and visions of the woman he'd encountered earlier replaying in his mind, Oliver dropped down onto the patio, falling onto his side as he landed.

Remaining still, he watched the back door. The lights were on in the kitchen, but from what he could see, the room was empty. Staying low regardless, Oliver hurried away, around the side of the property and in the direction of Stan's house.

Stan's backyard was not directly accessible, due to a stockade fence that surrounded the entire rear portion of the lot, so Oliver slipped into the space between their houses.

Running around to the front of Stan's house, he fell against their front door and stabbed furiously at the doorbell. Frantic, Oliver looked around every few seconds to make sure no one was coming, until the door opened and Stan's wife Melinda stood before him.

Dressed in one of her usual skimpy outfits, the kind even the coldest winter months were unable to dissuade her from parading around in, she looked as surprised to see him as he was her. She flipped the light on over the door.

"Turn that out!" Oliver growled.

Startled, Melinda switched if off. "What's the matter?" she asked in her typical squeaky voice. Normally comical, as it was better suited to a little girl, on this night Oliver instead found it unsettling. "You're all out of breath."

"Where's Stan?"

Melinda looked behind her then turned back to Oliver. At more than half Stan's age, with big blonde hair, heavy makeup, vacant blue eyes, and an over-the-top comic book heroine figure she'd crammed into a pair of skintight Capri pants and a scandalously low-cut top, she looked like a confused Barbie doll come to life. "Resting, he's not feeling good."

"Let me in, I—I need to talk to him."

"I didn't feel good before either," she told him, smiling to reveal big bright teeth. "But I'm all better now."

"Melinda, please, let me in! It's an emergency!"

"Okay—geez Louise—come on then."

As Melinda stepped away from the door, her stiletto heels clacking along the hardwood floor, Oliver looked around again to be sure no one had seen him, and then started inside. "Please, get Stan for me."

"I can wake him up," she said. "What's the trouble?"

"Just hurry, it's important."

"It must be if it couldn't wait. Soon as he felt better we were going to your place anyways."

Halfway through the doorway, Oliver stopped. "What? Why?"

"Well are you coming in or not, Oliver? You're letting all the heat out. Gilly gets mad something awful when I let all the heat out."

Oliver was about to back away when he saw Stan standing a few feet behind Melinda. His clothes were mussed, as if he'd just rolled out of bed. His arms hung loosely at his sides. In one hand he held a pistol.

"Oliver," he said softly, as Melinda moved out of the way.

"Stan, I—"

"Gilly," he corrected him.

"For Christ's sake, fine, *Gilly* then, I—"

"Good." Stan smiled a small and sad little smile. "Like I told you, that's what my friends call me."

Oliver stepped inside, closed the door and fell back against it. "I need your help."

"I know."

"You know?"

"There's nothing I can do, Oliver. I'm sorry."

"What's going on? You have to tell me, some—someone has to tell me!"

"Here's a little something you should know. I made a couple calls. That cop that came to see you isn't even a cop, least not any-more." He eyed Melinda, and although she seemed displeased about it, she walked away, disappearing into the shadows behind him. "Detective Brenda hasn't been a cop in a while, she retired few years ago. She's just driving the right car and using an old badge."

"What was she doing here then?"

"I don't know," he said. "I don't know anything anymore."

"Gilly, what's happening?"

"I was so sure I was right—same as you—but I…"

Oliver had never before seen him like this. Gone was the arrogance and edge, replaced instead with a palpable sense of helplessness, regret and sorrow.

"That's what it is, you know," he said softly, his eyes filling with tears. "People do things, they…they *believe* things because they think they're doing what's right…because they want to and need to be right, or what good are they? Even if they don't believe it at first, or realize they're wrong, they convince themselves they're right, they surround themselves with others who'll do nothing but reassure them how right they are. They think they're right. You see what I'm saying? People do things because they *think* they're right. We all do. We have to. Because we're all so frightened that by the time we realize just how wrong we might be, it's too late. Then what is there? What's left of us then?"

"Gilly, you—you've got to help me."

"I can't do anything more for you. I'm sorry…*truly* sorry."

"Look, I—"

"Run."

Oliver stared at him hopelessly.

With his free hand, Stan slowly lifted his shirt, exposing his belly and side.

He was wounded like the others. And the wounds were still bleeding.

"Run, Oliver," he said. "*Run.*"

14

Sticking mostly to the woods along the side of the road, Oliver managed to make his way out of the neighborhood undetected. After a mile or so, he'd reached the downtown area. He purposely avoided Main Street, finding a bus stop bench a few streets over. Collapsing onto it, he looked around, trying to catch his breath. The occasional car rolled by now and then. Otherwise the streets were empty. There was no one else in sight. Only a few blocks from his office building, a plan was already forming in his mind. He'd go into work, hide out at his office long enough to figure out what to do next, and make a move from there. There was a chance the others might look for him there, but probably not right away. At least in his office he'd be alone at this time of night—in fact, the entire building would be empty—and he'd be safe for a while.

Still exhausted and huffing, he forced himself off the bench and jogged toward his building. The air was cold and sharp, and as he moved through the empty, foggy streets, Oliver was certain he'd never felt more isolated in his life. Body spent and head full of madness, he pressed on, trying his best to exist in the moment and not let the horror of what was happening take hold.

Three blocks later, he reached his office building. It was dark, except for the lobby. With another quick look around, Oliver hurried through the front doors then made his way to the security desk and elevators beyond.

A young security guard he recognized named Freddy was work-ing the desk. He looked up from a paperback he'd been reading then put it aside and slowly rose from his chair.

"Mr. Young? What are you doing here?"

Oliver was happy but surprised to see him. Freddy normally worked the day shift. "Freddy, I'm so glad it's you, didn't expect to see you here tonight."

"I picked up some night shifts for extra money," he explained. "What's going on? You know you ain't supposed to be here."

"I know it's after hours but I need to get up to my office, okay? I won't be long. I just need to get up there for a few minutes."

"Come on, man." Freddy casually dropped a hand onto his belt. "You know I can't do that."

"I'm allowed to come in after hours. You just have to let me through. What's the problem?"

"For real?" Freddy frowned. "You need to go on home, all right?"

"I don't have time for this bullshit. Let me through."

"I'm just doing my job." Freddy sauntered around the side of the desk so that he was standing right next to Oliver. "You know that."

"I need to get up to my office, Freddy."

"Mr. Young, there ain't no office for you to get up to."

"What are you talking about? I work here."

"What's wrong with you?"

Oliver nervously looked around again. He needed to get the hell out of this lobby. It was well-lit and he could easily be seen from the street. "We've always gotten along, I—I always liked you, Freddy, I thought we were friends."

"I always liked you too, Mr. Young, you were always nice to me, treated me with respect, like I mattered. Not like most around here. And I appreciated it, believe me. Still can't let you through though."

"I don't understand. *What* is the problem?"

"The problem is you don't work here no more."

Oliver heard what he'd said, but it didn't register. "What?"

I know you don't want to get into it now, but things have been tough for you guys lately…

"I was really sorry for everybody that got let go when they made those cuts," Freddy told him, "but I still got a job to do here, and I need my job, Mr. Young, you feel me? I got a wife and new baby at home, I can't lose this paycheck. If I let you up there, it's my ass. Now you got no business here no more, and I'm sorry, but I got to insist you vacate the premises immediately."

God knows you've got nowhere to go or anything else to do…

Oliver slowly backed away. "I don't understand, I…what…"

The mail on the table…

"You ain't worked here in months, Mr. Young."

So much mail…

Standing in front of the desk, Freddy folded his thick arms across his chest. "It's time to remember now."

Bills they couldn't pay…

"It's time."

Oliver ran for the doors.

* * *

With no direction or intent, Oliver staggered along until he could barely stand. Leaning against the side of a building, his entire body ached and his lungs burned. He was down near the waterfront now, and the fog had grown heavier. There were no cars here, no one else on the street.

Stepping off the curb, he moved through the fog to the top of a large set of cement stairs. They led down to a paved pathway that ran the length of the canal below. In daylight hours the area was populated with walkers, joggers and others, but was now dark and wrapped in rolling fog.

There was a noise behind him.

Oliver looked back at the corner from which he'd come.

A young man stood watching him.

Partially concealed in fog and clad in dark clothes, his eyes possessed a crazed look, and two crosses were painted in what looked like blood on his face. On his left cheek, the cross was upside down. In his gloved hands, he held a crowbar. The man said nothing. He didn't need to.

Sore and exhausted, Oliver wouldn't be able to outrun the man, especially on the street. His only chance was to flee down the stairs and try to disappear into the darkness and thick fog below.

The man took a step towards him, and Oliver darted down the steps.

Descending into the darkness below, the fog following and the sounds of the man's footfalls close behind, Oliver nearly fell, but managed to grab the iron railing and steady himself about halfway down the stairs.

It was then that he saw the other two.

They were waiting for him at the bottom of the steps. Dressed in the same dark clothes and painted with crosses like the other man, one carried a club or some sort, the other a small torch, the flame contained but burning bright.

The one with the torch stayed where he was.

The other started up the steps.

Oliver frantically looked behind him. The man coming from the street was still several steps away, but coming fast. Gripping the railing with everything he had, Oliver waited until the man coming from the bottom got close enough, then pivoted his hips and threw a kick as hard as he could.

The bottom of his foot connected flush with the man's chest.

Grunting, the man fell backwards, tumbling violently down the cement steps to the path below.

Turning just in time to see the man from the street closing on him, Oliver ducked as the crowbar flew by, missing his face by mere inches. It hit the iron railing next to him with a loud clang that echoed eerily through the night.

With no other choice, Oliver ran for the bottom of the steps.

The second man waiting on him raised his torch, holding it with both hands, and swung it back and forth as if wielding a baseball bat.

Trapped, like the cornered animal he was, Oliver kept to a low crouch while looking for a way out. The man he'd kicked down the stairs was on all fours on the path now, but still hurt.

The other two inched closer, and in that horrible moment where he waited for the pain, the impact of the crowbar to crash down on him and the flame to burn him, Oliver saw something more. Several yards away, by the canal, the man in the fedora stood watching them, a ghostly silhouette wrapped in fog and darkness.

You coward, he thought. *You goddamn coward.*

A loud bang sounded, and the man in front of Oliver cried out, arched his back and turned, twisting as if in a frenzied attempt to reach his back. As he dropped his torch, another shot rang out and a chunk of his chest blew apart in an explosion of blood and flesh.

Oliver felt warm blood spray his face.

The man collapsed and lay still at the bottom of the stairs.

Behind Oliver, the man on the steps hadn't moved but was still watching.

Wiping blood from his face with trembling hands, Oliver staggered down the remaining stairs, stepped over the body and looked to the canal.

The silhouette was gone, if it ever really been there at all.

From the fog, another figure emerged.

Detective Brenda…

Arms locked out in front of her and a still smoking 9mm clasped in both hands, she inched closer into view. "We need to go," she told Oliver.

The man on all fours regained his feet, glanced at his dead comrade, then looked to the man still on the steps. Neither made a move for Detective Brenda.

"Oliver," she said, "*now.*"

Shaking violently and trying desperately to get his head around what had just happened, what was still happening, Oliver looked to her then to them, then back to her. With no idea what to do, he considered running again, but realized he wouldn't get far.

The men slowly retreated.

Silently moving back up the steps, they vanished into the fog.

Once satisfied they were gone, Detective Brenda lowered her weapon. "Are you all right?" she asked.

His face still specked with blood, Oliver shook his head no.

"Yeah," she said. "Right…"

"How did you find me?"

"Been following you for a while," she said. "I know how to do it without being noticed. I'm a cop."

"Not anymore you're not."

"We're like priests, child, once a cop always a cop. Let's go."

"I'm not going anywhere with you."

"In case you missed it, I just shot a motherfucker, saving your ass."

"You're one of them."

"Not yet."

"I saw the blood on your sweater when you were talking to Doc Adelson. That's why the other two left just now, why they didn't attack you too. You're one of them."

"I don't know how much longer I can hold out," she said, eyes twitching nervously. "I've been fighting it—*him*—best I can."

"The old man in the fedora…"

She nodded.

"What is he?"

"Older than Time itself, he's a fox in the hen house, a disease."

"How do we stop him?"

"I'm not sure he can be stopped."

"Why did you come to my house?"

"To find out what you knew, what Emily knew. I didn't know if she was too far gone at that point, so I pretended to still be on the job so you'd talk to me."

"And how did you know about what happened that night?"

She poked at the dead man with the toe of her shoe. "You're not exactly the brightest burning candle in the window, are you?"

"*Fuck you*, lady."

"I don't do sperm, darlin'."

"How did you know we'd hit the old man with our car that night?"

"How do you think?" Detective Brenda gave a heavy sigh. "I was there."

15

The bar was dark. A little hole in the wall located at the end of an alley, with no windows and low ceilings, it had the claustrophobic feel of a tomb. A few tables and chairs and a large scarred bar constituted the entire place. There were a handful of neon signs hung along the back wall, and a small TV was suspended in a corner above the bar. The only other person there was the bartender, an overweight middle-aged guy with cauliflower ears, a flattened nose and the facial scar tissue of a one-time boxer or wrestler.

Oliver had taken up position at one of the tables facing the door, the only way in or out, while Detective Brenda stood at the bar waiting for her order. On the television, the sitcom that had been playing went to commercial.

The lights from a cityscape appeared onscreen, as an announcer with the voice of a kindly grandpa straight out of Central Casting did the voiceover.

"It's midnight again in America..."

The bartender reached up and turned the sound down as an American flag appeared, filling the screen.

Oliver looked away.

Detective Brenda returned to the table with a bottle of Jameson and two shot glasses. "Have a drink with me, Oliver," she said, dropping into the chair across from his. The little beads in her hair sparkled and caught the nearby neon as she filled both glasses then slid one over to him. "We don't have much time, and I hate drinking alone."

Plucking a napkin from the holder on the table, Oliver wiped his face to make sure he'd gotten all the blood off. It was the third time he'd done it since they arrived. "Are we safe here?"

"We're not safe anywhere." She cocked her head toward the bar. Behind it, the bartender was filling bottles and paying them little attention. "I know him. Been coming here for years, he'll keep his mouth shut. So for now, we're good."

Oliver stared at the shot glass.

"Go on," she said, "get that up in you. It'll settle your nerves."

Oliver threw back his shot. It burned going down but felt good.

"Have you ever killed anyone before?" he asked.

"Ever seen anyone killed before?"

"No."

"Thirty years on the job, never fired my weapon in the line of duty."

"I'm sorry you had to fire it tonight."

"It's a dirty business, life."

"Is that what this is?"

"Whatever little's left of it."

"How did this happen?"

"It's terrible," she said, "the things fear can do."

"Is he some sort of vampire?"

"Fear always is." At closer range, Joan Brenda's big dark eyes were bloodshot and saddled with heavy bags. Even in low light she looked like she hadn't slept in days. "The dreams," she said softly. "The nightmares, they keep getting worse."

"Maybe they're not dreams."

"Maybe not…"

"Why don't I remember what happened that night?"

She filled their glasses again. "You're about to."

Up ahead, a lone figure at the edge of the sidewalk faces the street…

"Had an argument with my wife that night," she explained. "I needed to get out of the house for a while, so I went for a drive." Joan held her shot glass but didn't bring it to her mouth. "Came up on you when I got to Main Street, thought there might've been an accident. Your car was just sitting there in the middle of the street. Figured you might be in trouble, so I stopped to see if I could help. Old cop habits die hard, even the good ones."

Tall and thin, clad in a long coat to his ankles, a fedora atop his head, the man stands in profile, wrapped in fog.

Oliver drank the second shot as more images filled his head.

A silhouette, unnaturally still, like something manufactured.

"When I pulled over and got out of my car, I saw you sitting on the curb. You were wringing your hands and crying."

"Emily," he hears himself say.

"Your wife was on the ground, lying on her back in the street between your car and the curb." Joan swallowed the second shot.

The car swerves violently, and Oliver's head strikes the window.

"And the man...the old man, he was kneeling over her."

"Emily!"

"I was...crying," Oliver said, seeing it—seeing him, all of them, in his mind now. "I couldn't—I couldn't do anything, I—I wanted to, but I...I couldn't."

The blurred face of the man...a face of shadows...

"I thought maybe he was doing CPR," Joan said. "I didn't know what was really happening."

Not quite human...

"Or what was going to happen."

"He stepped right in front of the car," Oliver told her. "We hit him, and he was in the street. Then he got up. He stood up, I—I saw him. And then he looked at us and...and..."

"For Christ's sake, Emily, pull over!"

"And..."

Adjusting the fedora, he pulls the brim down in front.

"And then he *looked* at us." Oliver reached for his shot glass, realized it was empty, and let it go. "He..."

Turns and looks right at them.

"I was so frightened, I—we both were, I—I'd never seen her so scared."

Standing in the middle of the street, he watches them.

"Go, Emily," Oliver said, staring into the shadows between the tables. "I told her to go, to—I told her to go."

"She couldn't. None of us could."

He's in front of us now.

"How did…How did he do that? It didn't make sense, it—it wasn't possible but…somehow…he'd gotten in front of us and was standing in the way."

"We're going home," Emily says, trembling as tears stream across her face. "I want to go home now."

"And he's there, he's—*Jesus Christ*—he's at the door, he—"

"Easy." Joan poured two more shots.

Oliver tried to pick up the shot glass, but was shaking so violently most of it spilled before he could drink it. "He was right there. I looked into his face."

"Please," Emily cries, "God, please no!"

"That's when I knew he wasn't human."

"Stop, make him stop! He's touching me, I—don't want him touching me!"

Oliver slammed his shot glass down onto the table, the fear so strong he could barely stand it. Human beings weren't meant to be so frightened. "I don't know what happened, I—I can't remember what he did, I just know I was sitting on the curb and he was dragging Emily out of the car and I wanted him to stop I wanted him to leave her alone and she was screaming and I needed to help her and I couldn't and I—what is he what the hell is he and what is he doing he has to stop he needs to stop I want him to—you leave her alone you leave her alone!"

"It's all right," Joan said, reaching quickly across the table and taking Oliver's hands in her own. She gave the bartender a quick glance to let him know they were fine, then returned her focus to Oliver. "Oliver, *look* at me."

He did, his face a canvas of terror.

"I found you," she said. "I found you both. I tried to help, but I couldn't do anything either. It was like I was paralyzed. I just stood there and watched you cry because I didn't want to see what he was doing to your wife. I cried with you that night, Oliver, because I knew what was being taken from us, what we were losing, and in a way, it was almost as if by not stopping him, we were *giving* it to him. When he was done with Emily, he came for me. And I cried then too."

"Why couldn't I remember? Why couldn't Emily?"

"I didn't remember it all right away either. Maybe it's all too much for our brains to process. Maybe it's just another symptom of the disease—more of his bad juju, his evil—I don't really know."

"I'm going to kill him," Oliver said.

"He's not alive in the way you think."

"But he…*it*…is alive…isn't it."

It wasn't a question. She answered anyway.

"In the way terror is a living thing, I suppose so."

"Why did you help me tonight? Why me? Why now?"

"Felt like I failed to save you—all of us—that night. Maybe this was a chance to try to make it right, or at least as close to right as things are ever going to be again."

"It's not your responsibility to save us."

"Like I said, old cop habits die hard. Despite popular opinion, even though much of it's warranted these days, we're not all a bunch of murderers and thugs with guns and badges. Maybe it's just as simple as being the right thing to do. It *was* the right thing to do. Wasn't it?"

Gilly's words echoed in Oliver's mind.

People do things because they think they're right.

"I hope so."

We all do.

"Figured it was best to try while I still knew the difference," she told him.

"How bad *is* it out there?"

"Out where, Oliver?"

He knew what she meant.

Grimacing, Joan let his hands go and stood up. In pain suddenly, she gripped her side. Wincing, her breath caught in her throat, and she began to perspire. "We need to go, we—it's time to go."

Emily hits the gas, and Oliver watches as the shadow in the middle of the street recedes into darkness and fog.

"It's coming for us, isn't it?" he asked.

"It's coming for all of us, Oliver."

* * *

They stepped out of the bar and into the alley like the vagabond souls they'd become. The cold air brought Oliver back. His fear had settled. Or perhaps he was simply becoming accustomed to it, he couldn't be sure which.

At the end of the alley, across the street, Joan's car was parked, sitting dark and alone beneath an extinguished streetlight. She turned to Oliver. "This is where you get off, kid."

"Let me help you. You helped me, let me help you."

"There is no help," she said.

"I can't just leave you here," he said, reaching for her as another wave of pain struck, doubling her over this time.

She leaned just far enough away to remain out of reach. "Go, you...you need to go. The wounds are bleeding again."

"I'm not going to—"

"If mine are, they *all* are. We're all one, Oliver. That's what it knows that we've never been able to figure out. We're all parts of a single consciousness, like pieces of a larger organism, you understand? That can be a blessing or a curse, it all depends on who—or what—we allow to control it—*us*."

"There must be some way to—"

"You don't want to be around me much longer, Oliver." She glared at him. Something in her eyes had changed. "Trust me on this."

Deflated, he took a step back. "Where will you go?"

"Guess I'll find out when I get there, huh?"

He hoped he'd misunderstood her, but knew he hadn't.

"Try to stay in the light," she said. "It's the only thing that can cleanse fear. You know why? Because there's no such thing as the dark, it doesn't exist, it's a lie. There's only light, and the absence of light. In its absence, that *thing* gains power, thrives and spreads. We're all so afraid, but there's no reason to fear the dark or each other. It's the lack of light we need to fear. Instead of bringing more, we keep taking it away."

"Thank you for helping me, Detective Brenda."

She smiled wearily. "Joan."

"*Joan*," he said.

Oliver watched her walk through the trash and debris blowing about in the alley, and as she reached the street, she looked both ways then crossed and got into her car.

He hadn't yet made it to the mouth of the alley himself when through the car windows, Oliver saw several dark forms emerge from the backseat.

Joan turned and looked at him. As their eyes met, Oliver realized the shadows weren't attacking her. They were embracing her, caressing her and welcoming her to their fold.

Her eyes still locked on his, with another smile—this one defiant—Joan Brenda pulled her 9mm free, placed it under her chin and pulled the trigger.

16

Sparks flew like diamonds, rising and falling, living and dying in a shower both alien and graceful. Beautifully mesmerizing, they descended to the concrete in sweeping arcs one after the next, vanishing as they hit, the rain of cinder continuing to fall, replacing those extinguished with fresh sprays, a cyclical and brilliant fountain of embers burning through an otherwise dark night.

Oliver stood watching from across the street.

In a rundown gas station with a single-bay garage, the door open, a man in a welding helmet knelt over what appeared to be a large work of art of some kind. A dark and hideous tangle of humanlike forms, one an extension of the next so that they all appeared to be a single merged and horrifying entity, Oliver couldn't be sure if he was looking at metal or charred flesh and bone.

The man looked over at Oliver, as he knew he would, and raised the dark visor on his helmet. His hair hung long and loose past his shoulders, and even with a closely cropped beard, the deeply scarred and disturbingly weathered look of his face was evident. Eyes so dark they were nearly black glared at him through the shower of sparks.

It was the first person he'd seen since leaving the bar.

No more running, Oliver thought.

Very slowly, the man brought his free hand to his throat and dragged the tip of his thumb from one side of his throat to the other.

Oliver's hands tightened into fists.

Amused, the man smiled, revealing surprisingly bright white teeth. The canines, impossibly long and sharp, sparkled through the spray of embers like daggers.

Boldly, Oliver stared back.

The man lowered his visor and returned to his work.

Two blocks later, the streets empty, dark and quiet, Oliver came upon a small motel. Located next to an exit ramp, beyond, he could see the highway. Like the streets around him, it was oddly vacant.

Except for the light from the motel sign, everything was dark.

Oliver crossed the street, hesitating at the glass front door long enough to take another look around. No one...nothing...everything oddly quiet...

He slipped into the motel lobby.

Cramped and dated, it was empty but for a woman behind the desk. She stared at him, her face lifeless and void of expression. She held out her hand, extending it across the desk. A room key dangled from her finger. Her dead eyes never leaving him, the woman slowly cocked her head toward a hallway to her left.

Closing the gap between them, Oliver reached out and took the key.

The woman stared at him, saying nothing.

Oliver moved through the doorway and into a carpeted, dimly lit hallway. As he rounded the corner he was greeted by another larger, longer hallway.

Though just as dimly lit, this one was lined with people standing on either side, each one in front of a room door. A cross section of people from every walk of life, every gender and age and race, they stood blankly staring at him the same way the woman at the desk had. Oliver made eye contact with each one, to his left then right then back again, as he slowly drifted down the hallway and deeper into the motel. None of the people moved or made any attempt to stop or even engage him; they simply stared as he walked past, and while Oliver was afraid, he continued on, refusing to turn back.

As he left the hallway and crossed to another, to his right was a large glass panel that overlooked a courtyard and swimming pool below. Oliver looked down at the scene, his hand flat against the cool pane of glass.

Nude and bathed in moonlight, a long line of people, strikingly similar in both their diversity and ghoulish detachment, walked methodically down a series of steps at the edge of the cement pool. Walking until they disappeared beneath the surface, seemingly unaffected by the water, their eyes open and vacant, faces void of expression, they descended into the pool in a steady line, one after the next.

On the far side of the pool, another line of people emerged. Walking up steps at the other end, they arose from the water with the same blank look. But they had been transformed. Almost identical now, they stepped from the pool, walked across the surrounding patio then stopped, each in turn, and gazed up at the moon. After a second or two, they filed into a hallway that led to rooms on the first floor below.

Both lines kept moving, a seemingly endless procession of people descending into then emerging from the pool like some sort of demented assembly line.

Oliver looked to the moon. Each person stopped to look at it, as if they had some spiritual connection to it they hadn't realized previously. He stared at the brilliance of it hanging there in the sky and remembered how it had mesmerized him in his bedroom not so long ago.

The rest is dead, Oliver thought. *It's dead.*

Dying…

He continued on until he'd reached another hallway, this one shorter and empty. The lights sunken into the ceiling were mostly out, and those that were functional flickered on and off, coloring the hallway with a strange strobe-like effect. Oliver glanced down at his key. ROOM 180.

At the end of the hallway, on the left-hand side, Oliver found it. The key slid in, and he opened it, leaving it just ajar. A small amount of light spilled from within. A low, steady sound emanated from the heart of the room. It sounded like chanting of some sort, but he couldn't be sure.

Hesitantly, Oliver pushed the door open the rest of the way.

He could still hear soft murmurs, the cadence repetitive and solemn, like prayer, but there was no one there.

Don't be afraid, Oliver.

He looked back down the hallway. Flickering light…shadows…

Come and see. He stepped into the room. *Come and see…*

In the center of the room was what appeared to be a makeshift altar of some kind, and on it, a child lay on its back.

A baby…not human…at least not completely human…it couldn't be. Close—it was so close—but he'd never seen anything quite so beautiful, so breathtaking in its innocence and purity.

On its back, its little legs kicked slowly, as if for purchase, and the small arms extended, the fingers reaching for him so pale they were nearly translucent. The bald head turned, and a pair of striking emerald eyes blinked at him with slow, deliberate, ethereal simplicity.

Within them, Oliver suspected, if only one would look, was everything.

He reached down to the baby, and tiny delicate fingers curled around his index finger as the little hand took hold of him.

Oliver couldn't look away from those beautiful eyes. He didn't want to.

Not ever.

The baby, so quiet, continued to stare at him with what could only be love and grace so profound it made him weep.

This was connection…transformation…evolution…

Hope.

God in a sea of anger…

The baby blurred through his tears.

The little fingers released him, but the emerald eyes remained locked on his, telling him everything, and nothing at all.

Oliver wept.

Sinking to his knees, he felt those he could not see closing in around him. And somewhere not so very far away, just beyond the quiet chanting, there came a horrible laughter.

Like the sudden emergence of blood in water…

The cackling grew louder, echoed down the hallway behind him.

Death on the wind…

Creeping closer, it drowned out his cries.

And then, just as before, in the absence of light, Oliver was alone.

* * *

Even in his earliest moments of consciousness, Oliver knew he'd never been here before. He wanted desperately to be at home, but as his vision slowly cleared and brought his surroundings into focus, he realized he was in another room in the motel. The only light was a dull yellow hue emanating from a small lamp on the nightstand. Even beneath blankets, he shivered. Phantoms of mist, his breath floated free in ghostly columns, spiraling away through the dark room.

Despite the cold, Oliver rolled over, pushed aside the blankets and struggled into a sitting position. Groggy, he swung his feet around to the floor. As the shadows in the far corner shifted, he saw the silhouette of someone else.

Emily.

Her back to him, she sat on the bed next to his own, her knees pulled in close to her. Her spine, skeletal in the shadows, resembled an alien appendage. Protruding and snakelike just beneath her skin, it followed her lean torso all the way to her shoulder blades, disappearing behind her hair, which hung down around the back of her neck in an unkempt tangled mess.

Instinctively, Oliver reached for her, but she was too far away.

Slowly, she turned and looked at him over her shoulder.

Oliver had never seen such sorrow.

"It's all right," Emily said softly. "It's just you and me now."

"Where are the others?"

Her eyes slid to the closed door, then back to him.

"And the child?"

"Child?"

"The baby, Emily, where's the baby?"

She turned and crawled across the bed like a jungle cat, her nude body glistening with perspiration despite the cold.

At the edge of her bed she hesitated, gauging the distance before climbing across to his bed.

Nude as well, Oliver pulled the blankets in closer. He'd never been ashamed of his body, especially with Emily, but now he felt exposed and vulnerable, like an animal led to slaughter, throat unprotected and ready to be sliced. And perhaps it was.

"The baby in the other room," he said. "What happened to it?"

"You say the strangest things," she whispered, settling down next to him.

A strange aroma wafted from her. *Dirt*, Oliver thought. His wife smelled like freshly turned earth. Grimacing, he felt the emotion welling up in him as he looked into her eyes. This wasn't Emily. Not anymore.

"Am I insane?" he asked.

"Everything is a temporary state, Oliver. Even us. Even this."

He wanted to touch her, to put his hand on her cheek, to feel her warmth and familiarity, the softness of her hair, but he kept his hands in his lap.

"You haven't been yourself since you lost your job," she told him. "For months all you did was sit around the house watching the news, or surfing social media. You watched the world burn, and you—*us*—along with it."

"I remember what happened that night."

"I do too," Emily said. She smiled, but it was decidedly demonic. "It was already too late by then. He already had us, we just didn't know it."

Oliver brought his hands to his head, fighting the emotion.

"I remember lying on the street and how cold and hard it was," Emily told him. "How it smelled, the way his hands and breath felt on me, his mouth, his *teeth*—all of it—I remember all of it."

Eyes on the side of the road, watching from the darkness...

"I remember him biting me."

Slowly moving closer and closer into the moonlight...

"And I remember the others too."

Surrounding them...

"I remember when they came from the shadows to show themselves. I remember him—and them—drinking from me."

Touching them...

"Then I realized it was more than that." Emily told him. "They weren't just draining me of things I could eventually replenish, however diseased. They were *eating* me, Oliver. Devouring me... tearing me to pieces."

Feasting...

"But it's all right now," she said, reaching for him.

Her hands, so cold, moved slowly up and down the length of his arms, shoulders to wrist then back again, as she gently pushed him onto his back. Lying next to him, she let her cheek rest on his chest and looked up at him with something similar to love. Echoes now, ghosts of the things he'd once seen in those beautiful eyes.

"Emily…"

Sliding down, kissing his chest then stomach as she went, she nuzzled the soft flesh beneath his ribcage. Licking him first, and then kissing him, she slowly but forcefully pushed her mouth down onto him.

Oliver gasped as her teeth penetrated him. The initial pain dissipated faster than he imagined it might. Replaced instead by a strange tingling sensation, it was as if whatever was in her bite had deadened the area like Novocain.

As she fed, the door opened.

Others filed in slowly. There was nothing he could do to stop them now.

He wasn't certain he wanted to.

Emily stroked him as she drank, working him until he was fully erect.

The others circled the bed, waiting for their turn. Dark craters existed where their eyes should have been, yet they moved and acted as if they could still see…

His head whirled, and for a moment, Oliver felt nauseous. It passed quickly, but the dizziness remained. The room tilted and spun like a carnival ride.

"Don't be afraid," Emily whispered, finally pulling free of him, her fangs dripping blood across his groin, belly and chest as he came. "Fear blinds us…"

That's how they'll escape, Oliver…through your eyes…

Through the window on the far wall, Oliver saw the moon, so bright and high in the night sky. Slowly, the others closed around the bed until all he could see was their leering, ravenous smiles.

The jagged bloody holes where your eyes once were…

"But still, we see." Emily covered his body with hers. "We see through *his* eyes. And now, so will you."

The woods behind their house, the trees barren and towering over him like sentries long dead, the snow beneath his feet crunching as he runs, Oliver moves through the forest, staggering forward as best he can as his eyes tear and blur in the brutal cold, his breath flying all about him in thick clouds.

In the distance, through the trees, he sees their house, but it seems impossibly far away. He pushes forward, stumbling through the woods.

From above, a sudden and violent cracking sound...

Oliver falls against a thick tree, the bark cold and hard as granite, rough against his bare hands. The sound grows louder, and he looks up to the tops of the trees and the dead gray sky above.

Falling through the trees, crashing dead branches as he goes, the man in the fedora plummets to earth, his coat billowing like a cape.

Oliver drops to his knees, searches for something—anything to defend himself with.

A large rock partially protrudes from the frozen ground. Frantically, he begins tearing at it, continuing to loosen it even when his fingers split and bleed, until he manages to wrest it free.

I'm going to kill it.

The man in the fedora lands in a spray of snow and broken branches, his arms extended out on either side of him, head bowed. Even when he finally raises his head, the fedora is still pulled down enough to hide his features.

You can't kill it, Oliver.

The rock clutched in both bloody hands, he gets back to his feet.

It dies. Here, today.

With a primal scream of defiance and rage, Oliver charges.

You can only face it...

Raising the rock high over his head, he swings it with everything he has.

You can only become it...

Swings it toward the side of its head...

Become it, Oliver.

But there's nothing—no one—there...

Become fear.

And yet, as Oliver loses his balance and falls to his knees, the rock flying from his grasp and landing several feet away, bouncing harmlessly across the frozen ground, he knows he is not alone in these woods.

"Look at me, Oliver."

As her voice brought him back, the others in the room came closer, holding him down and pinning him to the bed.

"Become the things we have to show you."

Emily's hands gripped his face and held his cheeks tight. Her thumbs slid higher, finding his eyes then pushing, deeper and deeper still, even when he begged her to stop. Even when he screamed, and even when they burst in Oliver's head, running down his face in a milky and bloody goo-like substance that mixed with the crimson and cum still trickling from Emily's mouth.

17

The dream, it seemed, had saved him, if only for a little while.

Safe and warm in a small studio apartment on the top floor of an old brownstone in the Back Bay, books and records, spent beer bottles and empty pizza boxes everywhere, the curved windows overlooking the fire escape and the Boston Commons beyond, blurred and distorted through a steady rain, two college students lay side-by-side beneath heavy blankets.

"Why do you look at me like that sometimes?" Emily asked.

"I can't take my eyes off of you."

She wiggled closer, moving to his side of the bed. "What do you see that's so special?"

Oliver wished he could find the right words to express to her what she truly meant to him, how he'd fallen so hopelessly in love with her over these past few weeks, and how nothing mattered to him anymore—not college, not his friends or family—nothing but her. Instead, he kissed her. Gently, lovingly, he brushed his lips against hers. "You're the most beautiful woman I've ever seen," he told her. "And the most incredible human being I can ever hope to know."

"That's silly." Emily laughed lightly, blushing and looking away as she so often did when he complimented her. "So sweet I almost want to cry, but silly."

"Not to me."

"Even if I was, which I'm not, is that *all* you see?"

"Of course not..."

"What then?"

"I love you." Oliver felt his face flush. He had never told her before. He assumed, even hoped desperately that they both knew it, but they'd never said it. "I'm *in* love with you, Emily."

"Aren't you afraid?" she asked softly.

"Of what?"

Emily watched the rain as it spattered the windows and slid down along the curved panes. "The future, I guess."

"Not if you're in love with me too." He kissed her nose. "Are you?"

Her eyes met his, but she said nothing.

Oliver felt his heart drop. "*Aren't* you?"

Rescuing him, she smiled that same smile that always sent him reeling. Before the fear, the violence and death, there was only them, the rain, that smile, and a glint in her eyes that answered his question better than words ever could.

Oliver would try to remember. Even as the memories slipped free of his grasp and spiraled down into a cold and terrifying night without end, he would try.

* * *

Night had fallen. He could feel the dark. He slowly climbed the stairs and made his way along the dark hallway to the bedroom.

Standing in the doorway, a silhouette in shadows, he waited.

As a bank of clouds cleared the moon, a beam cut the darkness. He walked into the room.

On the bed before him, a long winter coat and a black fedora.

A wave of fear washed over him. One unnaturally familiar and oddly comforting, it flowed through him like the blood he could hear pulsing in his veins.

He slipped into the coat, pulling it in tight around him.

Then he reached for the fedora.

Carefully, he placed it on his head, pulling the brim down in front, trading it for the cover of shadows that had concealed his face prior.

Turning to the windows, he faced the moonlight and the night.

The blessed dark night…
He let it take him, and he and the darkness became one.

* * *

Moments later, not so very far away, Main Street was deserted and quiet.

As headlights appeared at the top of the street, he turned, and through new eyes, watched them creep closer from his position at the very edge of the sidewalk.

Behind him, in the darkness, the others waited.

Despite the cold, his breath made no clouds in the night air.

Oliver bowed his head as the car drew closer, illuminating him and the section of sidewalk on which he stood.

And then the man in the fedora slowly stepped off the curb.

Greg F. Gifune is a best-selling, internationally-published author of several acclaimed novels, novellas, and two short story collections. Working predominantly in the horror and crime genres, Greg has been called "the best writer of horror and thrillers at work today" by *New York Times* best-selling author Christopher Rice, "one of the best writers of his generation" by both *The Roswell Literary Review* and horror grandmaster Brian Keene, and "among the finest dark suspense writers of our time" by legendary best-selling author Ed Gorman. Greg's work has been published all over the world, translated into several languages, received starred reviews from *Publishers Weekly*, *Library Journal*, *Kirkus* and others, is consistently praised by readers and critics alike, and has garnered attention from Hollywood. Two of his short stories, "Hoax" and "First Impressions," have been adapted to film. His novel, *Children of Chaos*, is currently under a development deal to be made into a television series.

His novel, *The Bleeding Season*, originally published in 2003, has been hailed as a classic in the horror genre and is considered to be one of the best horror/thriller novels of the decade.

Greg resides in Massachusetts with his wife, Carol, a few cats, and a dog named Dozer. He can be reached online at gfgauthor@verizon.net or on Facebook and Twitter.

www.ingramcontent.com/pod-product-compliance
Lightning Source LLC
Chambersburg PA
CBHW051849170626
46807CB00003B/1406